Honor Thy Teacher

BY

TERESA MUMMERT

Copyright © 2012 Teresa Mummert

All rights reserved.

ISBN: 1477628797

ISBN-13: 9781477628799

Table of Contents

Chapter One

❧

"Fuck," I mumbled to myself as water droplets trickled down my face. I had spent my night out with Angela and was now running behind schedule. I grabbed a hand towel and patted my face dry as I looked at my reflection.

I was going against everything I stood for by being with a married woman. Not because I thought it was morally wrong but because I didn't like to share. In fact, I hated to fucking share. She reassured me her marriage was all but over. She and her husband barely acknowledged each other's existence, let alone slept together. I didn't believe her, but I didn't plan on being together long-term anyway. I was using her as much as she was using me.

I slipped into my bedroom and grabbed a pair of dark-wash jeans from my drawer. A small picture fluttered to the ground. I picked it up, purposely avoiding the image as I tucked it away in between my clothing. Thinking of what I had with Abby was too painful. She had been my everything.

I would have gladly dedicated my life to her, to our family, but she ripped those dreams away. I slammed the drawer closed harder than I intended, making the contents on top rattle. I ran my hands through my hair and made my way over to the closet, grabbed a blue dress shirt and pulled it on.

I was excited to be getting back to work. Teaching had always been a passion of mine, and part of that was due to Abby. She was my high school math teacher when we met. She kept me focused. I didn't realize my dream until college, when I took on tutoring others.

I didn't have to work at all, of course. My father is a prominent director in the movie industry. I liked taking care of myself. As much as I hated to admit it, it made me feel connected to Abby; even though whatever connection we had was severed some time ago.

I poured myself a mug of coffee and made my way down the stairs to the first level of my building. I'd converted a warehouse into a living space. It wasn't flashy and overbearing like most of the more expensive houses in the neighborhood, but it gave me the space I needed. A simple apartment would not do for my lifestyle.

I jumped into my black BMW and turned it on as I waited for the giant bay doors to rise behind me. My phone rang and I couldn't help but groan when I saw that it was Angela.

"Yes?" I snapped, not bothering to hide the irritation in my voice.

"I had an amazing time last night," she purred. Of course she did. I fucked her until she couldn't stand. I rolled my eyes. She came across as desperate, an extremely unattractive quality in a woman.

"I know you did," I replied coldly.

"When will I see you again?" she asked, practically begging. I checked my watch and smiled.

"Before you know it." I laughed to myself. I hadn't bothered to tell Angela that I was starting a new job at the college where she worked as a secretary.

I had received a call earlier in the week that a teacher by the name of Ms. Gibbs had to take leave for medical reasons. I was hired to take over her class, American Society and Culture. I could hardly wait to see the look on her face.

"Mmmm…You are such a bad boy," she teased. The things I did with Angela didn't even place on the scale of kink. For her, it was an awakening, but for me it was a way to pass an afternoon.

"You have no idea," I replied honestly. I drummed my fingers on the steering wheel, growing more bored with the conversation. It wasn't Angela's fault. No one held my interest in the way that Abby had. My lifestyle was drastically different since I had been with her. It wasn't until after Abby and I had split for good that I realized who I truly was. I'm a Dom. I need absolute control in every aspect of my life. Perhaps Abby was partly to blame for that side of me, but deep down, I knew that I was always meant to live this lifestyle.

Chapter Two

❧

I pulled into Kippling College right on time. I didn't have a first period class, but I wanted a chance to go over Ms. Gibbs' lessons before diving into my own. I said my good-byes to Angela and made my way into the main building.

I couldn't keep the smug grin off my face when I entered the office. Angela shot to her feet, and panic washed over her face. I smiled in her direction but turned my attention to another woman who was already at the counter. I exchanged words with her, while looking over her shoulder at Angela, who looked pale and nervous.

I left the office with the classroom keys in hand and headed toward my room. I heard the door to the office open behind me. The sound of her heels on the floor mirrored that of her frantic heartbeat, I'm sure.

"William?" she called in a loud whisper. I didn't stop, didn't turn to face her.

"Good morning, Angela," I replied as I made my way down the hall. I stopped in front of my classroom to unlock the door.

"Why didn't you tell me?" she asked as she followed me inside. "You can't be here!" Her voice was panicked.

I dropped my bag to the floor and spun around to face her. She backed up against the wall, her breath hitched. I stepped closer, my nose nearly touching hers.

"You do not tell me what to do. I will always do whatever the fuck I please. Is that understood?" I was clenching my jaw, trying to bite back some of the harsher words that had crossed my mind.

I tucked her hair behind her ear and ran my finger over her jaw line. She nodded, in utter shock. She didn't expect me to react the way I was, I'm sure. Why should she? As far as she was concerned, we were doing a little role-playing. She had no idea how far into the lifestyle I actually was. I'd never taken her upstairs. Never shown her where I really like to play.

"I-I'm sorry," she sputtered. For a moment, I felt sorry for her. I took a deep breath and ran my hands through my hair. It's one of my habits whenever if I'm upset, irritated, or frustrated.

"I'm the one who should apologize. It was unfair of me not to warn you. Do you forgive me?" I smiled sheepishly and could practically see her heart melt before my eyes. Her shocked expression shifted into a smile, and I knew I had her exactly where I wanted her. Angela was an open book. She was a liar and a cheater like all other women I encountered.

"Can we get together tonight?" she asked, leaning in toward me, begging me silently to kiss her. I pulled back, turning to retrieve my bag.

"I'll let you know." I walked over to my desk and didn't turn back to see her reaction. I already knew it was disappointment, and it was exactly the response I had wanted from her. After a few seconds, the door closed and she was gone. I blew out a deep breath. I needed to find a real sub. Someone who knew better than to talk back to me. Someone who took my word as law and didn't question what I did. Every move I made, every word I spoke was deliberate. Unfortunately for Angela, my heart didn't factor in to our arrangement. I was cold and uncaring.

The thoughts melted away as several students entered the room. I grabbed my notes and prepared for the class.

The day began relatively smoothly. I was getting back into the hang of things by the time the next period began. I hadn't taught for a few months, but it was second nature. The students filed in and made their way into their seats. I sat watching them for a few minutes, twirling a ruler in my hands as they chatted idly about partying. Class should have begun, but I gave them an extra moment or two to be seated. As I stood to speak, a lone straggler made her way into the class. She averted my gaze and slipped into her seat at the back of the room. She looked embarrassed, and something about that intrigued me. The way her long, dark hair framed her face and she innocently bit her lip did other things to me. This one was different. I could tell from the moment our eyes met. She didn't have an agenda. She wasn't looking to fuck everyone over for the greater good of herself.

"Now that we're all here, I'd like to introduce myself. Ms. Gibbs will be out for a few months for medical issues. My name is Mr. Honor," I explained. Several of the girls giggled and whispered amongst themselves. I could have any of them I wanted, but I didn't want them. That was a lie. I glanced back up at the dark-haired girl. Her cheeks flushed pink, and she quickly looked down at the papers in front of her. Pure submissive perfection.

I did my best to keep my mind on the task at hand for the rest of the period. When it was finally over, I couldn't empty out the room fast enough. I wanted to talk to her. I wanted to hear her speak.

"You, come here for a moment." I pointed in her direction. I settled on the edge of my desk as I waited for her to collect her things. I grabbed a ruler and absentmindedly flipped it in my hands. Her eyes watched my fingers intently. If she only knew what I wanted to do with those fingers.

"Yes?" she asked, her voice barely audible. She was nervous, or was she scared? She should be. She would drop this class and never look back if she knew what was good for her.

"What is your name?" I asked, desperate to hear her speak again. She didn't respond for a moment, and I had to keep from laughing. Did I really scare her that badly? Her face was a deep crimson now. I let my mind wander, thinking how her other cheeks would look that color.

"Emma. Emma Townsend," she replied, her voice shaking. I couldn't contain my smile any longer.

"Emma." Her name tasted sweet on my lips, and I wanted to know what it was like to say it under very different circumstances. "Please try to make it to class on time. Tardiness will not be tolerated. Next time there will be consequences." It was easy to slip into my Dom position with her. Too easy. I would have to make an extra effort to avoid her. Even as a master of control, I knew that would be too hard to do. I was in no position to be in control of someone so sweet.

"Yes, sir." Sarcasm filled her words, but they still sounded lovely. I wanted to hear her say it again. I wanted to hear her moan those words.

"Get to class, Ms. Townsend." Our eyes locked and I pleaded with her silently to leave. I didn't know how much longer I could pretend that I wasn't fantasizing about bending her over this desk. She must have received my message because she turned and left immediately. Perhaps she was just good at taking orders.

I couldn't wait for the day to end. My zipper strained just from thinking about Emma. I could hear her voice like a melodic song burned into my thoughts. I grabbed my work and made my way out of the classroom. My phone buzzed in my pocket. I pulled it out and quickly answered.

"What?" I immediately regretted answering.

"How was your first day?" Angela asked, obviously over our spat from earlier in the day. How was my first day? I honestly couldn't remember anything before it. My thoughts were consumed by Emma. "William?"

"A breath of fresh air," I replied as I exited out of the back door and made my way to my car.

"Want to celebrate?" she giggled and the sound reminded me of nails on a chalkboard.

"I'm exhausted." I slipped my keys into the ignition and glanced up just in time to see Emma cross the lot. Her shirt was white and hugged the curves of her body. Her shorts left little to the imagination. All I could think about was wrapping those long, tan legs around me. Just looking at her made me hard—not something that happened very often for me.

"Oh, come on. You don't have to do any work." She was whining. I drank in the last few seconds of Emma before she slipped into her old beat up car before responding.

"My place. One hour," I replied and hung up the phone before she could respond.

I watched as the cars filed out of the parking lot, making sure to slip in a few cars behind Emma. Her vehicle looked like it could break down any moment. At least that is what I told myself to justify following her home. We made our way to the poorer side of town before she turned down a short driveway to her house. It was a small home and not taken care of very well. The thought of such a beautiful creature living in such an abysmal dwelling made me nauseous.

I stepped on the gas and made my way back to the other side of town. I got my peek into her world. That is all I wanted. I promised myself after seeing where she lived, I would keep my distance, but how could I now? Now that I could see that she deserved so much more?

I was obsessing over someone I didn't even know. No one had made me so crazy since my ex. I shuddered at the thought. This wasn't the man I am. I don't care for people. I use them until I find someone new. Nothing had changed. Emma was just a distraction—a shiny new toy that I can't have, so I want her.

Fuck, do I ever want her.

Once I made my way across town to my home, I pulled inside the large garage bay and checked my watch. Angela would be here in twenty minutes. I grabbed my things and walked up to the next floor.

Grabbing a bottle from under the island, I poured myself a drink and drank it down. I ran my hands through my hair and poured another. A light knocking at the door pulled me away from my daydream. I adjusted myself before opening it.

"Happy to see me?" Angela purred as her eyes danced down my body.

She fucking wished. I forced a smile. Emma was something I could never have, and I needed to get my mind off her as soon as possible. Even I had enough morals left not to corrupt such an innocent creature. I turned back to the island and downed another quick shot before walking toward my bedroom. I didn't have to say a word. I knew she was following behind me like a lost puppy.

I closed the door behind her and began to undo my belt. She licked her lips, and I had to look away. Angela was using me to escape her reality, and I was doing the same. I just wanted to feel something—anything. I undid my zipper and sprang free from my boxers.

Angela immediately dropped to her knees and began to go to work. Looking down at the top of her head, her mass of blond waves distracted me, and I began to lose my erection.

"Something wrong?" she asked, looking up at me. I wrapped my fingers in her hair and forced her mouth back onto me. I tried to empty my thoughts and enjoy myself. I pushed her head harder against me and closed my eyes. Flashes of Emma crossed my mind. Her teeth digging into her bottom lip. The lips of an angel. Her long, dark hair framing her perfect face.

I gripped Angela's hair tighter in my fist as I grew painfully hard. I pushed deeper. She didn't struggle. She opened her throat and let me slide farther inside. She took me all in. As I came, I held still, pressed tightly against her lips as I let out a long, deep moan from the back of my throat. I glanced down at Angela who had a single tear streaming down her face, but she wore a proud smile. I buckled my pants and made my way out of the bedroom. Angela quickly followed, her hair in a knotted mess.

"You want to go out?" she asked as she ran her fingers through her tangled mane. I poured another shot and drank it down quickly.

"I'll see you tomorrow," I replied coldly as I drank back another. Disappointment clouded the room as she slowly walked to the door and let herself out. I poured another drink and ran my hands through my hair again.

What the fuck was happening to me? I made my way into the living room with my drink in hand. Settling on one of the leather couches, I grabbed my laptop and began searching for Emma Townsend. It wasn't hard to find her. The first social network I clicked on pulled up a full profile of her, complete with pictures. The sight of her made me immediately grow hard again. I clicked on her bio. She had a small number of friends. A few happy birthday wishes were on her page that she had responded to recently. It was her birthday? I thought of her sitting alone. I wondered if she had friends over, if her family was throwing her a party. I wanted to see the happiness on her face.

I don't know if it was the alcohol or my increasingly stalkerish behavior, but I was growing nauseous. I drank back my shot and closed my laptop.

Chapter Three

❦

I awoke late the next morning on my couch. I got up and grabbed my things. Checking my watch, I knew if I hurried, I could make it to work before Angela. She was the last person I wanted to see. Well, a close second. I took off my shirt and made my way into my room to grab a clean one.

I sped to work, hoping no one would be able to smell the lingering fragrance of alcohol on me. I avoided the office, knowing that as soon as Angela spotted me, she wouldn't leave me alone.

My classroom was empty, and I took a moment to straighten myself up and pull on my shirt. As I turned back toward the door, I could've sworn I saw Emma's beautiful face staring back at me. As quickly as she appeared, she was gone. I sunk down into my seat and rested my head in my hands. What was it about her? I barely knew her, and she had turned my world completely on its axis.

I was beginning to feel again, and it scared the shit out of me. I was in no position to care about anyone, especially someone I didn't even know.

The morning dragged on, and it felt like my first class would never begin. As students started to file into the room, I noticed Emma was among them. I had to look away so she wouldn't see my smirk.

Had she taken my warning seriously? Part of me wished she had been late to class so I had an excuse to keep her afterward. Not that being late in college was all that serious of a thing, still; it was the only excuse I'd need to spend a few minutes alone with her.

As much as I wanted to be alone with her, I knew it wasn't the best thing for her. I would allow myself to fantasize, but that was as far as it could go.

"Take your seats. It's time for a pop quiz." The room let out a collective groan. If a quiz was the worst part of their day, they could consider themselves lucky. The truth was, I wasn't sure I could fight off this hangover long enough to teach them anything.

I sat behind my desk and tried to do anything that would keep my mind off her. It was working for the most part, until someone dropped a textbook loudly onto the wooden floor. My eyes immediately met hers. She held my gaze this time, not looking down. She was biting her lip, and I was thankful I was sitting down and able to hide my growing desire for her.

I licked my lips, and her cheeks flushed. I immediately began to shuffle through the papers on my desk. I would have to learn to be in her presence without letting her have this effect on me. I was nothing more than a teacher to her. If she only knew the things I could teach her.

Time sped back up, and the class ended before I knew it. I was careful not to meet her gaze as she dropped off her paper and made her way outside the room. Fuck. I waited for the halls to clear before heading off to the men's room. I splashed some cold water on my face and avoided my reflection.

I couldn't get her out of my mind. I grew uncomfortably hard against my zipper. I slipped my hand down the waist of my pants and readjusted myself. The slightest touch caused a shockwave to ripple through my body. I wanted it to be her hand. I wanted to feel her against me. I gripped myself tighter and throbbed against my fingers.

The sudden sound of muffled laughter echoed through the walls. I pulled myself from my fantasy and splashed some more water on my face. The laughing grew louder, and I realized it was from the adjoining bathroom. I slipped out into the hallway and listened for a moment. The faint smell of marijuana filled the air.

"Girls," I called out in a commanding tone. The giggling ceased immediately. "Come out here right now!"

After a moment of whispering, the door finally opened. I almost fell over as I saw Emma staring back at me. She looked terrified but quickly gave way to another fit of laughter. I don't know what upset me more—her blatant disregard for herself or the fact that she laughed in my face. I clenched my jaw as I tried desperately not to slip into my Dom mentality.

"Emma? You think this is funny?" I narrowed my eyes at her and waited for a response. She stopped laughing and shook her head no, throwing herself off balance. I grabbed her arm and pulled her toward my classroom, hoping no one had seen her. Was she trying to ruin her life?

"You're lucky I don't have a class this period." I pulled her inside the room and closed the door, making sure I drew the blind on the window. She sobered up immediately. She looked scared. I didn't want her to be afraid of me. I needed to calm down. She wasn't my concern. If she screwed up her entire life, that had nothing to do with me. I ran my hands through my hair and took a moment to calm myself. I grabbed my ruler and spun it in my hands, trying to decide where to go from here. She bit her lip as she eyed the ruler nervously. Did she know what I wanted to do with it?

"What are you gonna do? Spank me?"

Fuck. She knew exactly what I wanted to do with it.

"You know, fifty percent of what people say in jest is the truth." I was rock hard just by hearing her say those words.

"Is that a fact?"

"Stop biting your lip," I said angrily, and slapped the ruler on the desk. She jumped at the loud crack, making herself bite harder. A thin trail of crimson dotted her pouty lip. Fuck. I had made her hurt herself. She really was scared of me.

"I'm sorry," she said quietly as her fingers touched her lip. *She* was sorry? I had caused her to hurt herself and she was apologizing to me. I walked toward her slowly, not wanting to alarm her. I needed to be closer to her, to make her feel at ease. I reached my hand up and slowly ran my fingers over her bloodied lip.

"Breathe," I whispered, leaning in closer. She pulled me to her like a magnet, and I was not a strong enough man to resist. We stood painfully close to each other, and time seemed to stop in her presence. I couldn't be sure, but I thought she felt it too.

Suddenly a loud ringing broke the spell. I dug my phone from my pocket. Angela was calling to make plans for tonight. I could barely hear her over the thudding of my heart in Emma's presence. I watched her as she watched me. Her cheeks had a slight touch of rose as she bit at her lip, an obvious nervous habit.

I narrowed my eyes at her, and she quickly released it from her teeth. A natural submissive. I grew hard again at the thought. She turned and wandered around the room, allowing me a moment of privacy to end my phone call. I let Angela know I wasn't feeling up to doing anything. Not with her at least.

I walked quietly up behind Emma, who was looking over some posters that hung on the far wall.

"You should get to your next class," I whispered in her ear as I drank in her flowery scent. She didn't turn to face me.

"So, I'm not in trouble?" she asked. If I didn't know any better, I'd have said there was disappointment in her voice.

"I didn't say that." I couldn't keep from grinning. She breathed deeply and nodded her head.

"Yes, sir," she replied as she grabbed her books and made her way back out into the hall. I ran my hands through my hair and laughed at myself. What the fuck was I doing? What the fuck was she doing to me? I slipped my hand inside the waist of my pants and readjusted myself. I knew exactly what she was doing to me. I walked out into the hall to clear my head. Emma stood talking with some friends, no doubt the ones who left her hanging, at the end of the hall.

"Get to class, ladies," I called out. Her friends quickly scattered, but Emma paused to look back at me. Her bright green eyes locked onto mine before she turned to make her way to her next class. I stepped back inside my room. I needed to get a grip on myself before I did something I would regret. She would regret. I swung at a stack of papers on my desk, sending them flying around me.

If Emma did like me, she wouldn't once she found out what kind of man I really was. I was incapable of getting close to anyone. I would use her, and when she got too close, I would hurt her. I had done it countless times before to countless women.

The difference was those women were no better than me. They lied, they cheated, and they used me as much as I used them. Emma was not like them. She didn't deserve to be treated that way, and I wasn't sure it was possible for me to treat her any differently.

Even if I could, what would she say when she saw the kind of things I really liked to do? She would be disgusted. I slammed my hands down onto the desk. I had gotten close enough, too close in fact. I needed her to know it could never go anywhere. I wasn't stupid. I had been with my share of women. I knew what was going on in her mind. She wanted me, but she wanted more of me than I could ever give.

The next few classes went by painfully slow.

As the day ended, I made my way out into the hall, watching as everyone filed by. Then I spotted her, and everyone else seemed to fade into the background. Emma was staring directly at me as her friends clung to her side. They were making plans to go out to the movies later that night. Emma agreed to meet them, and I shot her a quick smile before slipping back inside my room to grab my things. If she did like me, she wouldn't after tonight.

Chapter Four

❧

I drove home through the crowd of traffic as "Something I Can Never Have" echoed through the speakers of my car. Once again, I felt alone. Any happiness I had felt the past few days was gone. Emma would never look at me in any way other than a professor after tonight.

I climbed the stairs and quickly poured a drink. I drank it down and repeated the ritual a few more times before grabbing my phone and calling Angela.

"I knew you couldn't resist me," she purred. My stomach turned. I really needed to make time next week to find myself a sub, but for tonight, Angela would do for what I needed.

"Want to go out?"

She didn't respond immediately, and I contemplated hanging up.

"Yes!" she practically shouted, and I realized that taking her out for something other than a fuck was leading her on even more. I didn't care.

"Great. Be here in a few hours. Movie starts at eight."

"Want me to come by early? Maybe have a little fun first?" she asked. I thought about it. I had no reason not to continue to sleep with Angela, especially since I was planning to make Emma never want to look my way again.

"I can't. I have some things to take care of first," I lied. I ended the call and poured myself another drink. *"My dreams aren't as empty as my conscience seems to be."* The lyric played over and over in my head, taunting me. I needed to remind myself why I didn't want to fall for Emma.

Aside from protecting her from me, I needed to protect myself. I made my way into my room and pulled open my dresser drawer. Tucked away between the clothes was a picture of my ex-wife, Abby. She once was the most beautiful woman in the world to me, but now all I felt was hatred when I looked at her. She had chosen money over me, over our family. My eyes began to blur at the sudden memories that flooded my mind. Never again. I slid the picture back into the drawer and got ready for the night.

After a quick shower, I drank a few more shots. I took the elevator up to the next floor to remind myself of who I was. The room was dark and uninviting, a playground for a Dom. Perhaps I would bring Angela up here. Who knows, maybe she wouldn't be that opposed to it, and if she was, who cares? She was a dime a dozen.

I heard the doorbell echo through the building. I made my way back to my main floor and answered the door. Angela was beaming. I grabbed my wallet and ushered her outside before she could try to squeeze in a quickie.

"What are we going to see?" she asked as she placed her hand on my thigh. I glanced down at her hand and over to her. She drew back her arm quickly. I needed to calm down. Why was I wound so tightly? Maybe a quickie wouldn't have been such a bad idea.

"Slash," I said, avoiding her gaze.

"Well, you may have to hold me tight if I get scared." I could hear the hopefulness in her voice. Maybe this was a bad idea.

We pulled into the theater a good ten minutes before the previews. I paid for our tickets, and we made our way inside. The theater was still empty, so I chose a spot in the back row so I could watch as everyone filed in. Just before the lights dimmed, I spotted Emma. She was wearing a tight black dress and fuck-me heels. Her hair was curled, and all I could think about was wrapping my fingers in it. The lights dimmed and the previews began to play. Angela snuggled in closer to me, and I didn't pull away. It was nice to have the contact, even if I wished it were with someone else.

The movie wasn't as terrible as I had thought it would be. After a while, I got sucked into the plot, anxious to see what would happen next. I noticed some commotion up front, as Emma stood and tried to make her way through the crowd. It was now or never. I grabbed Angela and slipped out of the back exit into the hall. I pulled her up against the wall and began kissing her.

She didn't protest. I teased my way down her neck as she smacked me playfully on the chest. As my lips met hers, I opened my eyes to glance past her, and my gaze immediately fell on Emma. She bit her lip, and for a moment, I wished I hadn't come. I wanted so badly for my lips to be on hers. She looked hurt, and I knew without a doubt that she'd felt what I had. She disappeared into the restroom, and I used the opportunity to get myself out of there. She had seen enough to know I wasn't worth her time.

Chapter Five

❧

I took Angela back to my place and told her I had a migraine. She offered to stay and take care of me, but I assured her I would sleep it off. After she had left, I checked the time. The movie would just be ending now.

I poured a drink. I couldn't get her off my mind. I was starting to scare myself. She reminded me of who I used to be. Back before Abby had destroyed everything that I was.

Abby was the picture of perfection. She made me care about myself, my future. I fell for her quickly. I knew how easy it was for someone vulnerable to fall for someone in a position of power over them. I needed to be careful not to do that to Emma. Look what it got me. I lost the one person I had loved…to greed.

My father paid her to break my heart, and she took the bait. The saddest thing was our unborn child, who was lost in the process. I poured another drink and downed it.

I was too damaged to ever be anything to anybody else. I barely knew Emma, but she had awakened feelings in me

I hadn't known I was still capable of having. I couldn't ever be that person again.

I *wanted* to be that person again.

I grabbed my phone and scrolled through the contacts. I hit the call button and waited for an answer.

"William, what are you doing? You can't call me this late." Angela's hushed panicked tone brought me back to reality. She wasn't concerned about how I was feeling. She didn't get butter-flies at the sound of my voice. I was nothing to her. The feeling was mutual. I hung up the phone and tossed it on the couch. I needed to get out of this fucking place.

I grabbed my keys and some cash and made my way down-stairs to my car. I needed to regain control of myself. I needed to remind myself what I was.

I drove across town to the edge of the city to a seedy strip mall that had long been forgotten by most. A few cars dotted the parking lot. I whipped behind the building and parked my car. As I walked across the dark lot, I hit the lock on my Beemer and walked inside.

The main lobby was dimly lit, and three women sat on their heels, heads bowed in a row, by the front desk.

"Mr. Honor. What a pleasure to see you, sir," the voluptuous brunette behind the desk greeted me. I nodded politely as my eyes danced over the kneeling women.

"The usual, sir?" she asked, and my eyes shot up to meet hers. I nodded and made my way back the dimly lit corridor. I was in my element. I felt whole again inside these walls. I stopped in front of door three. A bulb glowed red just above the frame. I took a deep breath and stepped inside. I quickly unbuttoned my shirt and slid it off, draping it over a bench in the corner, followed by my undershirt. I slipped off my shoes and socks and slid them under the bench as well. I was ready. The door opened a few minutes later, and a small-framed brunette slipped inside. She was wearing a black see-through teddy and mile-high heels. I dropped to my knees, resting on my heels.

"Good boy," she praised me. I took a deep breath and relaxed. My life thrived on having control, and when I felt lost, I handed that control over to someone else. It was therapeutic.

She walked around me, her finger running along my shoulders. She traced the lines of the tribal tattoo that wound its way down my arm. "You know what makes a good Master, William?" she asked as she made her way to the front of me. I didn't answer, didn't look up at her.

"You may respond." I took a deep breath and thought about her question.

"I don't think I know anymore," I replied honestly. She bent over and grabbed my chin in her hand, jerking it up toward her.

"Respect," she said simply and let go of my face. She walked over to the shackles that hung from the corner of the room. "Come," she said. I rose to my feet and stared at the floor as I made my way to her. She grabbed my left arm and locked it into place above my head. "You respect me as your Mistress and give me control over you." She grabbed my other arm and raised it above my head. "I respect you and would never do anything to you that you don't want," she continued as she clicked the cuff into place.

"Not everyone will understand this lifestyle, William, and not everyone is cut out for it," she explained as she undid the buckle of my belt and slowly pulled it toward her. She leaned in closer so I could feel her breath on my ear. "You are."

I pulled against the restraints. She noticed, and her hand came across my face swiftly. "Is there a problem?" she asked, her voice cold. I clenched my jaw and resisted the urge to respond. I knew she was trying to provoke me to make me accept my true nature, but I refused. "Very well," she said. Her eyes burned into mine. She let the belt slide through her fingers and onto the floor. She walked across the room to a table full of toys and ran her hand over several of them before choosing a flogger to her liking. It was black leather with metal beads at the end of each tail. She smacked it mindlessly across her palm as she made her way back to me. Her fingers made quick work of the shackles as she freed my hands. "Remove your clothing."

I slid my jeans and boxers over my hips and let them pool at my feet on the floor. Her gaze fell to my waist as she eyed my cock.

"What seems to be the problem, William? Don't like the lack of power?" she stepped closer and ran the flogger over my chest and down the ridges of my abdomen, slapping it lightly against me. When I didn't respond, she used her free hand to grip me tightly, slowly sliding up the length of my shaft. My body betrayed me, and I flexed against her involuntarily.

She smiled, proud of her ability to make me hard. Her eyes darted to the prayer bench across the room. "Bend over." I dared a glance up at her, not moving. She clenched her teeth and lowered her voice. "Take your punishment like a good little bitch, or I will use the cane."

I narrowed my eyes but walked to the bench. I would not give in. I folded my body over the leather top, resting my hands above my head. Her heels clacked against the tile floor as she followed me.

"I never realized what a pussy you are."

I gripped the edge of the bench until my knuckles turned white. She brought the flogger down swiftly across my backside in three quick motions. A low growl resonated from my chest, and she stopped. "What seems to be the problem?" The flogger came down again, this time with more force.

My mind went blank, and I flipped over, grabbing her wrist before she could strike again. A hint of a smile played across her face as she fought to regain control. I backed her up to the four-post bed and pushed her backward, landing hard on top of her. There was no denying how much I enjoyed the power as I pressed against her inner thigh. I gripped both her wrists with one hand and pulled them above her head. I reached between us and ripped the black lacey fabric of her panties.

"I knew you had it in you," she said with pride.

I squeezed tighter on her hands as I pushed hard against her entrance, sliding inside her with one powerful stroke.

"Now I'm in you." I thrust again as she moaned loudly, throwing her head back in pleasure. She wrapped her legs around my waist to allow me to go deeper. Her heels dug into my ass as I thrust again. I slipped my free hand around her throat, squeezing as our bodies bucked against each other.

Her walls tightened around me, gripping me from the inside. She whimpered as her release came. I found mine moments later, collapsing on top of her.

I grabbed my clothes and got dressed, then left the room without a word. I left quickly and headed back to my place.

I felt renewed and as if I had a better grasp on who I was again. Seeing things from a sub's perspective made me a better Dom.

Chapter Six

I awoke as a new man. I got up and made my way to the gym on Thirty-Second Street to start my morning. I made my mind up that this evening, after work, I would start taking applications for a new official sub. I had tried my hand in the dating world, but it was more of a hassle than anything else. I was still holding a lot of resentment toward Abby and just didn't have the right mentality for anything other than a Dom/ sub relationship.

Emma had officially been removed from my every waking thought and so had Angela for that matter. At least that's the lie I told myself.

I spent the next hour working up a sweat on the treadmill and lifting free weights.

I took a quick shower in the locker room and headed over to the bistro on the corner for some breakfast. I placed my order with the petite blond waitress. There was nothing extraordinary about her. She was attractive, yes, but looked exhausted. Still, something about her caught my eye. As she tipped her head to fill my mug with coffee, I realized who she was. She was much different not kneeling naked in the middle of a lobby, but I was certain it was her. When she glanced back at me, her cheeks were pink, and I knew that she had recognized me as well.

"Thank you," I said as she finished.

"You are welcome, sir," she replied with a wicked grin and turned to make her way behind the counter. Maybe I wouldn't have to go through an application process after all.

Chapter Seven

❧

J made my way to work early. I needed to see Emma and reassure myself that I felt nothing for her. She triggered something inside me that I still hadn't worked through with Abby. That was it. That is what I told myself all morning. I also wanted to gauge her reaction toward me after the scene at the movies. I wanted to know that she didn't care.

Angela was trying her hardest to corner me so we could talk. There was nothing to talk about. I couldn't give her what she needed, and she couldn't give me what I needed. I wasn't even sure myself what that was.

When it was finally time for Emma's class, I sat at my desk, twirling my ruler out of habit. I watched the class slowly fill, and there was no sign of her. For a moment, I thought she was running late so I could keep her after class. I quickly pushed that thought aside. I eventually had to start the lesson. My stomach was twisting in knots. I just wanted to know she was OK. I decided I was going to skip out of the last few classes of the day. I needed more time. My head still wasn't right, and Emma, present or not, was fucking me up beyond repair.

As I stepped inside the office, my eyes first locked on to Angela's, who was blushing and twirling her hair as she saw me. I smiled at her politely, all too aware of the smell of flowers that consumed the air around us. Emma. There was no escaping her. I made small talk with Angela and quickly turned to leave the office.

"You missed my class. Come see me after you're finished," I said, locking eyes with Emma. My gaze dropped to the white bandage around her arm. I knew if she came to my class that she understood what was going to happen. Part of me hoped she hated me and didn't show.

I made my way back to my classroom and sat down at my desk. This part of the wing was deserted this time of day. Just then a light knock rattled through the door.

"Come in," I called. Emma opened the door and walked inside. I began to unbutton my shirt, leaving on my black undershirt. I folded it and put it over the back of my chair. "What happened?" I asked, glancing down at her bandaged hand.

"I had an accident," she replied nervously, biting her lip. If she didn't want this she would have run by now. She was screaming for discipline, for someone to take control in her life.

"I saw you at the theater yesterday. That was…" I said as my eyes danced up and down her body.

"Awkward," she replied, finishing my sentence. I couldn't help but laugh.

"Unexpected," I corrected her. Another lie. "Ms. Townsend, do you remember what I said about being late to my class?" I asked, sitting down on the edge of my desk and waiting for her response. After a moment, I gestured for her to come closer. She sat her books on a desk in the front row.

"I'm really sorry. It has been a crazy morning and..." she began to explain. I had no tolerance for excuses. It was obvious to me that Emma lacked discipline and had no regard for her own personal safety. She needed to learn. I wanted to teach her.

I grabbed her and bent her body over my desk. I brought my open hand down hard across her backside. Before she could protest, I brought it down again. I leaned over her, covering her body with mine.

"Shh...You need discipline," I whispered as I gently rubbed her backside. She relaxed underneath me. I took a moment to get control over my breathing. I stood upright again and smacked, this time harder. "You have no self-control," I continued. She gripped onto the edge of the desk as I continued to punish her. She was enjoying herself. "You need someone to teach you how to be a good girl. Someone to punish you when you are bad."

I was struggling not to cum at the very thought of fucking her. No one has ever made me feel so out of control while being completely in control. *Fuck.* I rubbed gently over her where I had struck her. She pushed back against my hand as I let my fingers dip between her legs. She wanted more. I smacked her one last time. She was panting heavily as she lay sprawled out across my desk. She was beautiful.

"Get to class," I panted. She lay still for another moment. I circled the desk and began putting back on my shirt. After a moment, she regained her composure and stood upright. I came back around and grabbed her books, holding them out to her.

She took them, unable to look me in the eye, and left the room as quickly as she could. I sat down on the edge of my desk to catch my breath. I was wrong. There was no forgetting about Emma. She had pushed her way into every fiber of my being, and I couldn't get enough of her.

Chapter Eight

Everything that had happened over the last few days had evaporated. My thoughts were consumed with Emma. I promised myself I wouldn't touch her. I promised myself I wouldn't hurt her, but now it was inevitable. I completely lost control of myself, and it felt incredible and heartbreaking at the same time. I had already forgotten my last lesson. Respect. If I respected Emma, I would have let her live her life free of me.

I made my way down the hall to leave for the day, lost in my own guilty thoughts.

"William!" Angela called from just outside of the office.

"Fuck," I cursed under my breath. "Not a good time, Angela," I said, checking my watch to show her I was in a hurry.

"It will only take a minute. Let me walk you to your car." She joined my side, and we continued out to the parking lot. "Look, I'm sorry about the other night," she began. My eyes quickly followed the scent of flowers that filled the air. Emma was perched on the curb, leafing through her textbooks.

"Don't be sorry," I said coldly. I didn't care. Angela didn't even register on the scale of things I gave a shit about. Right now, all I wanted to know is why Emma was sitting on the curb looking sad and forgotten. Where was her car? Had she wrecked it? Is that how she injured her arm?

"I don't want you to be angry with me, William." Angela looked genuinely concerned about my feelings. Too little, too late.

"I'm fine. All good things must come to an end," I said and kissed her lightly on the cheek. She stared at me for a moment, her expression blank. She struggled to regain her composure before she smiled and went to her car. I waited for her to pull out before heading back across the lot toward Emma, who was deeply engrossed in her book.

"No ride?" I asked, startling her.

"My aunt is hit-and-miss when it comes to responsibility." She looked like she wanted to say more but stopped short. She lives with her aunt? I wanted to know more. Where were her parents? Why wasn't she driving? What the fuck did she do to her arm?

"I never miss." Her green eyes burned into mine. "Come on. I'll take you home." I turned and made my way back across the lot. I didn't give her a chance to think about it. I wanted to be alone with her so I could find out more.

I opened the door for her and took her books. She looked like she was questioning whether or not to go with me. Part of me wished she would say no. *That's right. Run the other way.*

She didn't run.

She slipped delicately into the front seat. I threw her books onto the backseat and slid in beside her. I was getting in way too deep with her, and I knew it.

I sped out of the parking lot, trying to place as much distance between us and prying eyes as possible. As we reached the light, I realized she wasn't wearing her seat belt. Thoughts of her injured arm and missing vehicle filled my head. I leaned over her, inhaling the delicious scent of flowers as I grabbed the seat belt and pulled it across her body.

"Wouldn't want you to get hurt." I had to smirk at those words coming from my mouth after I had bent her over my desk and spanked her. "What happened?" I asked glancing down at her bandage.

"Long story," she replied, averting her gaze. I had no patience for games. I was already pissed enough that I even cared.

"What happened?" I asked again, this time with irritation in my voice. I wasn't asking; I was demanding a response. She sighed heavily.

"I drank a little last night. I knocked down a picture and accidentally cut myself trying to clean up the mess," she explained, holding up her hand. "No big deal." Her words dripped with sarcasm.

I whipped the car to the side of the road, and before she could say anything, I had unbuckled my seat belt and was facing her. A bee drawn to the sweet nectar of a flower. My mouth hovered over hers, and her breathing quickened.

"Do not talk to me like that. It pisses me off, and you don't want to see what I do when I am pissed off." I was beyond angry. I stared at her for a long moment before gently running the pad of my thumb against her cheek and down over her bottom lip. I couldn't be angry with her. There were a million things I could be with her—anything she wanted. "You don't want this," I whispered, with warning in my tone.

"Yes I do," she whispered. I slipped my hand along her neck and back into her long, thick hair. I couldn't help myself. I needed to feel her.

"You don't have any idea what you are getting yourself into," I stated. She licked her lips and let them slowly part. I had no control over myself any longer.

"Please," she begged, and my body gave way to carnal need. I gripped my fingers tightly in her hair and pushed my lips hard against hers. I slid my tongue slowly inside, and she pushed back against it with her own. She moaned as her hands began exploring my body. She arched her back toward me, and I soon wouldn't be able to stop myself from fucking her right here along the busy street.

"We can't do this here." I struggled to catch my breath. I hoped she wouldn't ask me to take her home.

"Where?" she asked as she pushed her lips against mine again. *Fuck.* I captured her bottom lip in my teeth.

"My place." I pulled back from her to gain my composure. I kept my fingers laced in her hair, tugging gently. "I have to explain some things before this goes further," I warned her. She bit her lip and nodded.

"You have no idea what that does to me." I released her hair and pulled back out onto the highway. *Maybe she was just looking to be my sub. Maybe it was nothing more than physical attraction. I could fulfill those needs for her, couldn't I? At what risk? If I was the one who got hurt in the process and not her, I could live with that. I was owed bad karma from countless indiscretions. It would be worth it to be with her.*

Chapter Nine

❧

We pulled up in front of my warehouse a few minutes later. She looked frightened, and I realized I should have warned her that I didn't live in a normal home. We pulled inside the large bay door, and it closed behind us, encapsulating us in darkness.

I got out and quickly made my way to her side of the car and opened her door. I couldn't wait any longer. I needed to feel her against me. *This is what she wants,* I told myself. I pulled her from the car and pressed her back against the cold metal. My hands wandered down her back. I grabbed her ass and pulled her body tight against mine. I wanted her to feel how badly I wanted her. My lips brushed against hers. "You can say no at any time."

She bucked her hips against me, and I struggled not to throw her on the hood of the car and fuck her right here.

"Do you understand?" I asked, breathing heavily.

She nodded her head yes, her breathing rapid and shallow. I slipped my hand up and wrapped it in her hair, tugging harshly.

"Do you understand?" My lips brushed across her earlobe, and I felt her body shiver against me.

"Yes," she purred into my ear. I pushed my hips into her again.

"Yes what?" I wanted this to be perfect. I wanted her to be mine, completely.

"Yes, sir" Her words shot through me like electricity. I bit lightly on her earlobe.

"Good girl." I forced myself to pull away from her. "Follow me." A million thoughts ran through my head, all of them Emma.

I held her arm in my hand as we made our way up the stairs, not wanting to break the physical connection between us. This was what she wanted. She wasn't thinking of me day and night, as I was about her. She wanted the one thing I could give to her. She wanted to lose control.

However, I hadn't picked her up at the club. She couldn't possibly know what she was asking from me. I needed to explain things to her. I had had this conversation before. Sometimes, they would give in and want to play; others would leave and never look back. *What would I do if she left? What if she runs away?* The thought made me sick.

I pulled out my keys and unlocked the deadbolt, pushing the door wide open. I wanted her to see that I wasn't living in an abandoned warehouse. I had made it my home. It was warm and inviting—the walls a rich brown with eclectic artwork dotted throughout.

"Not what you expected?" I asked, waiting for some sort of reassurance that she was OK. She nodded, a smile hinting at the corners of her mouth. She noticeably relaxed. I closed the door behind her, locking it. I reluctantly released her arm.

I walked into the kitchen area with her footsteps echoing behind me. She stopped on the opposite side of the island and watched as I dug around in the cupboards. I pulled out a bottle of scotch and two small glasses. She eyed me curiously as I filled them.

The truth was it wasn't for her. I needed the liquid courage to keep from pulling her into my arms and saying things I would later regret, breaking her heart.

"Oh, I can't," she said with the wave of her delicate fingers. I slid one of the glasses toward her.

"You will need this," I said as I drank my shot, hoping she wouldn't notice the slight tremble of my hands. I wanted to throw her down on the island and have my way with her right here. *Maybe one day,* I thought. *Not today.* She grabbed her drink and gulped it down quickly, making a face as it passed her lips. I refilled the glasses.

"I have very particular tastes," I said as I swirled the brown liquid in my glass before drinking it down. She drank hers, this time her expression unchanging. She glanced around the room.

"I like your taste." She tucked her hair behind her ear.

"That's not what I meant." I smiled at her innocence as I refilled the glasses. "I like to be in control," I explained, hoping she would understand. "But I will never do anything you don't want me to do." I could see her withdrawing slightly. I walked around the island and cautiously placed my hand on her neck, sliding my fingers down over her chest, stopping just before reaching her breasts. Her body responded as she arched her back toward my hand. I wanted to force myself to stop, but the pull to her was far too great.

"I understand," her voice rang through with false confidence. It was understandable; I was nervous as well. She bit her lip.

"If you understood, you wouldn't keep biting your lip like that." My body involuntarily pushed flush against hers. Her hands snaked their way to my chest, and she began to fumble with the buttons on my shirt. *Oh, God. How had I not noticed the innocence in her before? I knew she wasn't like the others but...*

"Have you ever done this before?" I asked as I tried to swallow the lump that was forming in my throat. I searched her eyes, hoping I had misread her.

"I don't make it a habit of sleeping with my professors," she replied, sarcasm dripping from her words. Behind that, there was nervousness.

"That's not what I meant." I could tell she understood but didn't want to say the words.

"No," she whispered, looking down at the still fastened buttons of my shirt. I pushed back from her, needing space in between us. I had never even considered the fact that she was a virgin. Very few at her age are.

I tried my best to hide the horror in my eyes as I thought back to bending her over my desk. I must have been unsuccessful because she immediately folded her arms over her chest, her face wrought with rejection. I wanted to protect her, to make that sad expression fade away.

"Look at me," I pleaded with her. She didn't move, staring blankly at her feet. "Look at me," I said again, more commanding. I reached out hesitantly and tipped her chin up with my fingers. She didn't recoil at my touch. As her eyes met mine, I froze, not wanting to say what I was about to say. I took a deep breath and forced the words to leave my mouth. "I can't do this." The words stung, and she flinched. My mind raced at the horrible mistake I had made, letting myself give in to what I felt for her. Tears welled in her eyes, and reflecting back at me was the monster I had become.

She pushed past me, heading toward the door.

I had no right to try to stop her.

"I'll find my own way home." Her voice cracked under her sadness. I followed after her, grabbing her arm and forcing her to face me. She needed to know it wasn't her fault. She needed to know I was a monster, and she should be thankful that it didn't go any further. She trembled under my fingers as tears began, slowly, to fall down her cheeks. I froze. I couldn't find the words to tell her how I felt. I was a coward.

She pulled free from my grip and left my apartment.

I didn't chase her. I let her go.

Chapter Ten

❦

I walked back over to the island, wanting to numb myself from everything that had happened. Corrupting Emma was a new low. I poured myself a drink. As the liquid burned my throat, I chased it with another. I thought of Emma, outside, alone. *I can't let her out there by herself. Not after what I have just done to her.* I grabbed my laptop and quickly searched her name. I pulled up her profile on the Facebook page I had found the other day. I scanned her info and saw her number. I dialed it, not second-guessing myself.

"Come get me," she said, the sadness still evident in her voice. She obviously hadn't expected me to be on the other end.

"Where are you?" I asked, wanting to run to her, to comfort her. I was selfish for even considering it.

"Like you care." She was angry, and the words stung. I couldn't leave her out there with no way to get home.

"I just want to make sure you make it home safely." I struggled to hide the frustration in my voice. As much as

I wanted to make sure she was safe, I wanted to see her. I was a wolf after an injured fawn. Not even I could stop myself from hurting her.

"I'm not going home. I'm going out," she hissed, and the line went dead. I had rejected her, and she was going out to find comfort in someone else's arms. I cursed under my breath, clenching my phone so tightly that my knuckles turned white.

I made my way back to the kitchen for another drink. *Why do I care what she does and whom she does it with?* I had let her leave. I was a vile creature in her eyes. That is what I had wanted. My phone rang, and I felt the sadness wash away. She changed her mind. I grabbed the phone and held it up to read the caller ID. It was Angela. My heart sank.

I poured another drink as I thought about answering it. Soon, the apartment filled with silence. I quickly dialed Emma again. I needed to know she was all right and wasn't going to do anything stupid because of me. It rang three times before a voice answered, but it wasn't Emma.

"Hello?" a female asked. I could barely hear her over the thudding of the music in the background.

"Is Emma there?" I asked, hoping I had the right number.

"She's right here. You should hang out with us. We're at The Rapture," she giggled, slurring her words. I heard a man's voice in the background, and I could have sworn he said Emma's name.

"Perhaps," I replied as I ended the call. I knew I shouldn't go, but Emma obviously had a low tolerance for alcohol, as evident by her injured hand. I couldn't live with myself if someone else took advantage of her. *Could I live with myself if I took advantage of her?* I didn't want to know the answer. I grabbed my keys and went after her. I told myself I just needed to know she was all right.

I sat in the parking lot at the club, trying to convince myself that I had no right to care. If I went to her, everyone would see me. I wouldn't be able to show my face at the college again. I gripped the door handle. Just then, Emma stumbled outside of the club. I breathed a sigh of relief, yet I was angry at her state of inebriation. I grabbed my phone and hit redial.

"What?" she asked bitterly. I deserved her anger, but it didn't make it easier to take.

"You look like you've had too much to drink." I said, frustrated with her lack of self-control. Coming from me, it was laughable. I got out of my car and leaned against it, watching her. Her eyes quickly scanned the parking lot, coming to rest on me. I couldn't help but smile.

"I can take care of myself, but thanks for your concern," she spat angrily.

"I'll give you a ride." I tried to hide the growing frustration in my voice.

"Fine," she replied before hanging up. She walked toward me, and my smile grew wider. I wanted to take her in my arms right there, but instead, I opened the passenger door.

Chapter Eleven

She looked uncomfortable. Her arms were wound tightly around her waist.

"Have fun?" I hated to see how self-destructive she really was. It made me ill.

"I had a great time," she bit back. She wouldn't meet my gaze. "Where are we going?"

"Back to my place. You need to eat something." She needed to sober up. She couldn't go back home wasted and depressed. I needed to protect myself. At least that's what I told myself. I knew I really wanted to make sure she was OK. I had nearly barged into that club, career be damned. Even with the slight buzzing of alcohol coursing through my veins, I knew I was willing to risk everything for her.

"I need to call my aunt. If she comes home and I'm not there…" She pulled her phone out of her pocket. I reached over, placing my hand on it before she could dial. The touch of her skin against mine, however slight, sent a shock through my body. Her eyes grew wide. She had felt it too. I swallowed hard, pushing what I felt deeper.

"Send her a message. Tell her you are staying at a friend's house. It won't look good that you're hanging out with your professor," I said. Her eyes stayed fixed on mine. She nodded and reluctantly withdrew my hand. She quickly typed out a message and slipped the phone back into her pocket. We rode in silence for the remainder of the short drive to my place.

As we pulled inside, I sat for a moment, contemplating my next move. *Give her something to eat, and then take her home. She is not yours to worry about.* I was determined not to hurt her again.

I exited the car and waited for her to join me. I motioned toward the steps, placing my hand on the small of her back as I guided her upstairs. My pulse quickened at the feel of the muscles in her back.

As we stepped inside, I was careful to put some distance between us. I quickly went to work at preparing her something to eat. *What do angels eat?* I thought as she settled in on a bar stool across the island.

She picked at her sandwich, ignoring the glass of water. I pushed the glass closer.

"Thank you," she said quietly. I ran my hands through my hair, trying desperately not to focus on her mouth as she ate. I grabbed my bottle of liquor and filled my glass. She ate in silence as she watched me slip further and further away. "I'm sorry… about earlier." Her eyes fixated on her food.

"I'm the one who should be apologizing," I replied, shaking my head. "I should have never brought you here. I can't do this to you." Saying the words aloud felt like a dagger in my chest. I took another drink. She pushed back from the counter and headed toward the door.

"You said that already." Her voice was small, and she was on the brink of losing it all over again. I followed her, not letting myself think of the consequences. She opened the door, and I pushed it closed from behind her. I had to explain. I couldn't let her think any of this was her fault. I had preyed upon her like an animal. She turned slowly to face me. I was close enough to feel the heat from her body. A single tear slid down her cheek. *I am an animal playing with its food.*

"I didn't say I don't want to; I said I couldn't." I wiped away the tear with my thumb. She didn't pull away from me. Her expression changed from wanting to escape to pure wanting. She grabbed my hand in hers and held it against her face. She felt it too. "You don't want this," I whispered as she moved closer. Her hands left mine and she slowly began to undo the buttons of my shirt.

I knew what I was about to do was wrong, but I couldn't resist her anymore. This time, her hands were steady. She pushed the shirt from my shoulders, letting it fall to the floor below. I grabbed the bottom of my undershirt and pulled it over my head. My eyes never left hers. I began to undo my belt as her hands slid across my chest. I folded it over in my hands and undid my button, letting my jeans sag low on my hips. I didn't care about the consequences. I wanted her. I wanted to fuck her. "You're being a very bad girl." The hint of smile played at the corners of her mouth.

"What are you going to do to me?" I could hear the nervousness in her voice. I grabbed her uninjured hand and lowered it to my zipper. I pushed against her so she could feel how much I wanted her. She gasped but didn't pull away. I leaned in closer to her ear, letting my lips brush against her.

"I'm going to punish you."

Chapter Twelve

⁂

*H*er hand flexed against me, and I almost fell to my knees with her touch. I began to slowly rock against her as her hand moved delicately over me. "That's enough fun for you. Now it's my turn." I wanted to dominate her. I wanted to make her feel things she never had imagined. I wanted her to let go and to give her pleasure over to me. I led her to my bedroom at the far end of the floor. "In here I am in charge. In here you belong to me." Her eyes danced over the bed. "We will take it slow at first."

I walked toward her slowly, praying she wouldn't run away. I put my hands on either side of her face and slowly leaned in to kiss her. She didn't pull away from me. After a moment, her body relaxed against mine, her lips parting, giving me entrance. Her hands raised, and she trailed her fingertips down my stomach. I grabbed hold of her quickly. I wasn't ready not to have full and total control. "You can't touch me unless I tell you to. Understand?"

She understood completely. She willingly sacrificed herself to the wolf.

My mouth found hers again, and we picked up where we had left off. I slipped my fingers under the hem of her shirt. She gasped aloud at my touch but didn't stop me. I was waiting for her to pull away at any moment, but she didn't. I pulled my mouth free of hers to watch her as I slowly circled her stomach with my fingertips. Her body vibrated beneath me. I pulled the shirt over her head and stepped back to drink her all in. She hadn't worn a bra. That was an unexpected bonus. She crossed her arms over her chest, trying to hide herself. "Move your arms. I want to see you." I regretted my tone, but she did as I asked. Her arms fell, reluctantly, to her sides. She caught her bottom lip between her teeth as she looked at the floor. "Look at me," I ordered.

Her eyes met mine, setting my entire body on fire. I stepped closer to her. I traced the top of her jeans with my fingers, allowing them to dip slightly out of sight. Her gaze never left mine as I slowly leaned closer, using my lips to brush the delicate skin of her neck. She shivered beneath me as I explored her further with my tongue. I made my way to her breasts, sliding my mouth over one of her nipples as I undid the button of her jeans. The sound that escaped her mouth was the most erotic noise ever uttered. I looked up at her as I repeated the flicking action of my tongue. She was slowly unwinding and on the brink of ecstasy. Her fingers wound into my hair and tugged gently.

"Bad girl," I scolded her. "I know how we can fix that." I had been dying for this moment. I didn't like it when anyone broke the rules, but I knew what would come after would be sheer bliss. I licked my lips at the sight of her playing with the belt in my hands.

"Lie down." I motioned toward the bed.

She didn't hesitate. She slid her body past mine, making sure to brush her naked chest against mine. She crawled across my bed, lying in the center.

I couldn't look away. I followed her, crawling over the top of her body, careful not to rest any weight on her. I slid the belt slowly over her stomach and lightly over her chest. "Give me your hands."

She placed them in front of me. I looped the belt around them and pulled them above her head, securing them to the headboard. I wanted to feel her hands on me, but I couldn't. I couldn't let anyone touch me. It would hurt too much in the absence of their hands. "That's better," I whispered in her ear. I trailed tiny kisses down her jaw as gooseflesh followed. My mouth found hers quickly. *This, I could allow myself.* Her tongue pushed back against mine, and my hips involuntarily bucked against her in response. I had her right where I wanted her, and she had me.

I slid my hands lower, pushing at her jeans, careful to leave her panties in place. I didn't want to push too much too soon. I thought of the fact that I didn't give her a safe word. I didn't want to scare her. If she told me to stop, I would, without hesitation.

I lowered myself, kissing my way down her chest, paying special attention to her hardened nipples. She began panting, her chest rising and falling hard beneath my lips.

"Shhhh…" I whispered against her. I slid my hand lower, rubbing over the delicate fabric of her panties. She melted under my touch. A deep moan escaped her throat. I stilled immediately. "I warned you." She looked pained, longing for me to touch her again. I lifted myself off her. I wanted to show her the release of complete submission. "Roll over," I commanded. But she didn't move. "Now!" I hissed.

She flipped over onto her stomach. I slowly slid her jeans over her hips and threw them across the room. My hands had ached to touch her. I slid them over her bottom, as I struggled not to cum at the very sight of her. I allowed my fingers to dip between her legs, and her breath hitched.

As she took another breath, I brought my hand down across her backside. She shrieked at the sudden contact. "Shhh…" I warned her, testing her. I brought my hand down again. She didn't make a sound, and I couldn't help but smile proudly. I rubbed over the pink mark and kissed it gently. I swatted her one last time. She remained silent. I leaned over her and whispered in her ear, "Good girl."

I unzipped my jeans and pulled them off, anxious to be closer to her. "Now, you get a reward." I lowered my body onto her, placing myself between her legs. I pushed against her, and to my surprise, her body pushed back into mine. "You want me?" I asked, hardly able to speak.

"Yes," she panted, and my hips flexed against her.

"Yes what?" I needed to hear her say it.

"Yes, sir," she moaned. I had to pull back from her. I wouldn't be able to stop myself from finishing if I didn't.

"Not yet," I replied, as I forced myself to leave her. She tugged at the belt that bound her hands. "Roll over," I commanded. She didn't hesitate this time. She rolled back over to face me. I waited for the shock to wash over her as she gazed upon me naked, stroking myself. "Spread your legs," I commanded. She slowly moved her legs. "Wider," I yelled, a little harsher than I intended. She did, her eyes never leaving my hand. I searched her eyes for any sign of fear, any sign of regret. There was none.

I crawled over her, positioning myself between her legs. I rubbed over her panties, mirroring the action of my other hand.

She pushed back against my fingers. Her eyes closed. I began to quicken my pace. "Look at me." My voice was low and came out as a growl. She gasped but didn't make another sound. I leaned in and brushed my lips across her inner thigh. She squirmed beneath my lips. I held her legs in place as I moved my mouth along her panty line. I slid them to the side and slowly began to tease her with my tongue. Her body arched and pushed back against me. I slid my finger inside of her, preparing her for me. I continued to work over her with my tongue as I moved my finger more rapidly. As her hips steadied their rhythm with my finger, I slid another inside of her. I could feel her walls tightening around me as her sweet juices filled my mouth. Her body shook below me as pure pleasure swept through her. I withdrew, licking the juices from my fingers as I crawled up the length of her body. "You taste amazing. I want you to taste how amazing you are." I kissed her hard, forcing my tongue inside her mouth. I knew she would resist, but I didn't care. In here, I was in charge. In here, it was my rules. She struggled against my mouth as she pushed against me. I grinded my hips harder against her. She bucked against me, now returning my kiss forcefully. I looped my fingers in her delicate yellow panties and pulled, causing them to tear apart in my fingers. I pressed against her, letting her feel me at her entrance. I kissed her, moving painfully slow. Her body tensed around me. I held still waiting for her to relax a little more. I kissed her slowly, tenderly, until I felt her grow more at ease, slowly rocking her hips toward mine. "Harder?" I asked, not wanting to hurt her more than I knew I would. If not here in the bedroom, then later when she realized what kind of man I really was.

"Yes," she moaned, arching her bottom into me. I pushed again and again until I was fully inside of her. She tugged on the belt, and I was glad I had secured her tightly. I suddenly stopped, stilling myself inside of her as I caught my breath. I pulled out of her as confusion washed over her face. I grabbed a condom from my side drawer and made quick work of putting it in place, wanting desperately to be against her again.

"If I get too rough, you need to let me know." She bit her lip and nodded, but I needed to hear her say it. To make sure she understood. "Answer me!" I commanded. I pushed against her, teasing her.

"Yes, sir," she moaned. I couldn't control myself as the words spilled out of her lips. I entered her fully, needing to feel her around me. I reached between our bodies, rubbing her, desperate to feel her walls tighten around me again. It didn't take long. She bucked against me as I kept pace, wanting to ensure she was pleased. It occurred to me that it had been a very long time since I had put someone else's pleasure before mine. She tightened around me, and I pushed harder, finding my release in time with hers.

I collapsed onto her, reaching up lazily to untie her hands.

Chapter Thirteen

❦

I pulled myself off her and put on my jeans, running my hands through my hair. *What had I done?* I allowed myself to steal a glance at her. She lay sprawled out on my once white sheets, rubbing her wrists gingerly, the small spattering of crimson marring the vision of an angel. I grabbed her clothing and tossed them to her, not wanting to look at what I had done any longer.

I grabbed the small, torn piece of fabric that was once her panties and slipped them into my dresser. I left the room without glancing back at her. She deserved better.

I poured a drink and swallowed it quickly, running a hand roughly through my hair. I sickened myself. Just as I was wallowing in my own self-pity, two delicate arms wound themselves around my waist. My stomach turned at the intimate contact. I wanted to apologize to her, to beg her forgiveness, but the words wouldn't come. "Don't," was all I could manage.

"Did I do something wrong?" she asked. Her words cut through me. *How could she think she did something wrong? What kind of fucking monster was I?* I couldn't breathe. I drank down another shot. My mind raced as my body grew numb.

"I'm going to go. I don't live far from here." Her voice was muffled compared to my own thoughts as I cursed myself.

The next sound I heard was the sound of the front door closing, and Emma was gone. It was the middle of the night, and I was so wrapped up in my own misery that I let her leave.

Without a second thought, I chased after her. I got in my car and made my way down the main road. It took only a moment to see her, a perfect fallen angel walking amongst us unworthy humans. My headlights created an angelic halo around her. I hated myself for prowling after her. I told myself it was for her. It wasn't safe for her to be out at this time of night. The truth was it was less safe for her with me.

"Get in," I yelled. But she began to walk faster. "Get in," I called out again.

"Fuck off!" she yelled at me, her face full of disgust. I slammed the car into park, my anger beginning to boil over. I jumped out of the car, wearing only my jeans. She stopped, looking at me as if I scared her. I should. "Leave me alone!" She pushed passed me. I clenched my fists and went after her.

"Let's go!" I said, grabbing her arm and pulling her toward the car. *Why was she being so goddamn stubborn? Did she not know what kind of men were on these streets? I was on these streets.* I opened the door and waited. She quit fighting against me and slid inside, defeated. I closed her door and made my way around the car. Clenching my jaw, I slammed the door behind me. She jumped at the sound. I took a deep breath, trying to calm myself down. I didn't want to scare her.

"I shouldn't have let you leave," I said, trying to sound calm.

"Which time?" she asked, her words filled with hatred. I gripped the steering wheel tightly, trying to keep my composure.

"I'm no good for you, Emma." She looked at me, holding my gaze briefly. I hoped she could see the regret in my eyes.

"Yeah, I get it. You don't want me." She was on the verge of tears. Her words hurt. It was like a slap in the face. Something I deserved.

"I don't want you?" I couldn't help but laugh darkly. "Emma, I just had you." She had no idea how badly I wanted her—more from her than I would ever allow myself to take. "Is that what you wanted for your first time? Some person tying you up? Fucking you and humiliating you?" I was disgusted with myself.

"That's obviously not what I pictured but I...enjoyed myself," she replied shyly. Her words traveled through me, stirring something primal inside of me.

"I know you did." She bit her lip and tucked her hair behind her ear. *What the fuck am I doing?*

"It's not like we couldn't try it again." Her face flushed red. I swallowed hard. I couldn't let her make this mistake again. I shook my head. She grabbed for the door, ready to run.

"Emma!" my voice came out panicked; I grabbed her arm, desperate to keep her from leaving. "I didn't mean I don't want to do it again; I just can't give you what you want. I can't give you what you deserve. What happened back there is all I know. There will never be anything more than that with me. I do not get close to people. I don't care for people," I lied. *I was a fucking liar and a coward.*

"Then why are you here? Why not just let me walk home?" She could see right through me.

"I don't know," I replied, letting her arm slip from my fingers. *I knew what she wanted to hear. A fucking coward.*

"Good night, Mr. Honor." She slipped out into the darkness.

"William," I called after her, wanting to show her she was right about me, that deep down somewhere she had broken through. There was something different about her—something special.

"What?" she asked, turning back toward me.

"My name is William. Please get back in the car. It's not safe out here for you." I would never forgive myself if something happened to her. She stood there, deciding which fate would be worse. "Please." My pulse quickened as she took a step closer to the car.

We rode silently through the city as I took her to her aunt's house. I relished in the last few minutes of smelling the flower scent that lingered around her. Her house was empty and dark, but Emma didn't seem fazed by it.

"Thanks," she whispered as she exited. I couldn't look at her. I probably would be the cause of years of therapy for her.

I pulled back onto the road, turning the radio up to drown out my own conscience.

"I really miss your hair in my face and the way your innocence tastes."

A lumped formed in my throat, and I switched off the radio and rode home in silence. I couldn't give her anything but heartache.

Chapter Fourteen

❦

I awoke on the couch, reaching out for someone who wasn't there. I couldn't bring myself to sleep in my bed alone. I ran my fingers through my hair and stumbled into the kitchen, pouring a cup of coffee. I looked around for my phone and realized I had left it in my car last night. As I opened the door, a tiny scrap of paper fluttered to the ground. I picked it up and flipped it over in my fingers. I read it over. As the words sank in, I let it flutter to the ground. I sprinted to my car and immediately began calling Emma. Her phone rang endlessly. I ran back up the steps, grabbing the note as I pulled on clothing. I needed to make sure she was OK. If anything happened to her because of me, I wouldn't be able to live with myself.

I made it across town in record time. Emma's driveway sat empty. I called to be sure, but she didn't answer. I banged on the door, hoping that she was OK. The door flew open, and there she stood, looking slightly shocked and absolutely delicious.

She was wearing nothing but an oversized T-shirt. I had to take a moment to regain my composure.

"William?" My name sounded sweet across her lips.

"Are you OK?" I searched her face for any sign of distress.

"I'm fine," she said as she walked into the kitchen. I reluctantly stepped inside, not wanting anyone to see me. "What's wrong?" she asked as she prepared her breakfast.

"Why didn't you answer my calls?" I was growing frustrated with her calm demeanor. *Was she ignoring me on purpose?*

"I was going to as soon as I ate something." She held the spatula up to show me she was, in fact, busy. "Why are you here? If my aunt was home, she would call the police!" I watched her pull out an extra plate, so I knew I was right that no one else was home. Her shirt lifted as she reached in the cupboard, revealing her small cotton panties. I felt myself grow hard. I cleared my throat.

"I parked down the street. Has anyone come by here? Anyone who seemed strange?" She didn't seem to take my urgency seriously.

"Only you," she joked.

I rolled my eyes at her and took the extra plate of food from her hand. "Why? Is someone looking for me?" she asked. I tried not to look too worried. I ran my hands through my hair and let out a deep sigh.

"I can't stop thinking of you."

Her eyes met mine, and I could think of nothing else. She flushed red and looked away.

"Look at me." She had no idea how absolutely beautiful she was. When her eyes met mine, I couldn't keep myself from touching her. I stroked her cheek with the back of my hand. She didn't recoil. She bit her lip, and it sent restraint to the wind. I found her lips with mine. My fingers laced through her hair.

"We can't," she moaned as I kissed a trail down the hollow of her throat. I turned her around, bending her body over the table. The cotton panties peeked out from under her shirt.

"You better show me your room before I fuck you right here." I traced the line of her underwear with my fingertip.

"OK," she panted.

"Good girl," I whispered into her ear before pulling back and allowing her to stand. I followed her down the narrow hallway, anxious to touch her again. I was drunk from her beauty. I could no longer resist the pull she had on me.

As we reached the doorway, I couldn't hold back. I lifted her and carried her inside, kicking the door closed behind us. She wrapped her arms around me, and for once, I didn't recoil at the touch. I laid her down on her bed and began to undress. She watched me with large doe eyes, biting her lip as she waited for me to touch her again. I took in the length of her legs as I undid my belt. She was perfection.

"You have no idea the things I want to do to you." The words burned as they left my lips. She really had no idea the things that ran through my mind. I struggled internally not to become that person with her, but there was nothing I wanted more.

She reached for me, letting her fingers glide down my stomach. Clearly, she knew she was breaking one of my rules. I captured her wrists in my hand and forced her back onto the bed, coming to rest on top of her.

"I like it when you fight."

She bucked her hips against me. I gripped her tighter, forcing her hands above her head. *Submissive perfection.* I secured the belt around her wrists and took a moment to admire her. "That's better." I smiled at her as an amused grin played across her face. I ran my fingertips down the length of her body. When I reached her hips, I gripped them tightly and pulled her toward the edge of the bed. She gasped at the sudden movement. I only wish I could have seen her expression when I flipped her over onto her stomach. Her body folded at the hip as her legs hung over the edge of the bed. I lowered my pants and took my time slowly peeling her panties off her backside, letting them fall around her knees.

I brought my hand down across her backside. She gripped the blankets in her fists and whimpered. I struck again, this time entering her before she could catch her breath. She moaned. I didn't stop her. I snaked my hand up to her mouth and muffled her cries with my fingers. I thrust into her rapidly, without compassion. Her body went stiff beneath me. I made sure she heard how pleased I was by her. Her tongue ran across the length of my fingers. I bit gently on her earlobe as my fingers slipped into her mouth and she sucked them gently. I moved in rhythm with her mouth, pushing her farther as my other hand gripped her hair. I felt her begin to tighten around me, and I was dangerously close to cumming.

"Emma!" a voice called out from the other end of the house. I clamped my hand tightly over her mouth as her body shook below me. I slid painfully slow inside of her and held still, listening.

"Shhh…" I breathed in her ear as her body finally stilled beneath me. "We will finish this later." I quickly undid her hands and began to get dressed. She lay motionless before me. I pulled her panties back up her thighs, followed by kisses.

"Go see what she wants before she comes back here." She reluctantly got off the bed. Her eyes fixed on my chest. "We will finish this later," I promised her as I watched her turn and leave. I pulled on my shirt and walked over to her bedroom window. It was already unlocked. I'd have to remember that. I glanced at a picture of her that looked to be a year or two old. She was smiling and sitting in the sun; her long, dark hair hung perfectly around her face. I slipped it into my pocket before I climbed outside and made my way down the road to my car.

I sat with my hands on the steering wheel, clenching it tightly, trying to convince myself to leave. My phone vibrated in my pocket.

This is a bad idea.

My heart sank in my chest as I read the words. I was too far gone to be denied her any longer.

It is too late for that. Are you alone?

I hoped she wouldn't turn me away. I could still feel her against my skin. I couldn't imagine not feeling that again.

I'm in my car.

She didn't say no. I needed to see her.

Where are you?

The grocery store near my house.

I will be right there.

I couldn't drive fast enough to be closer to her. My obsession with her was making me sick. There was no way around it now; she was going to get hurt, and it would be by my hands. If I had any compassion at all, I would have driven the other way.

I pulled into the grocery store parking lot and searched for her car. It was getting harder and harder to breathe.

Chapter Fifteen

As soon as I saw her, I couldn't take my eyes off her. She stared at me expectantly. I knew the damage was already done. I didn't deserve her.

"Are you OK?" I asked, walking slowly, hoping she didn't turn me away.

"I'm fine."

I released the breath I didn't know I was holding and took her face in my hands. I kissed her softly on the forehead. I could tell something was bothering her, but I was fairly certain it was not me.

"I'll get your things. Wait in my car." I clenched my jaw as I thought of what must have transpired between Emma and her aunt. I grabbed her purse and headed back to my car, willing myself not to care. I knew she was having doubts about us now. Her text messages replayed in my mind.

"Find everything?" she asked as I slid her purse into the backseat. I nodded, not wanting her to see the anger that boiled under the surface. It made me sick that anyone would hurt her. I tucked her hair behind her ear. The irony of my thoughts was not lost on me. I hoped one day she would confide in me. I wanted to know why she was so self-destructive. I had always been reckless with my own life, but I couldn't bear to see her destroy hers. Perhaps that's all I was to her—a way to destroy herself.

We rode in silence. She stared out the window at all the people in the streets. Emma's face looked sad and like she was a million miles away. I placed my hand on her leg to comfort her. I could have said something to make her feel better, but words failed me. I was too lost in wondering why it bothered me so badly. I don't like to see any woman hurting—not outside of the bedroom, at least. This was different, and it fucking scared me. I was struggling to convince myself that the attraction I had was purely physical, but watching her sad and withdrawn had stirred up emotions in me that I didn't know I was capable of feeling.

My mind quickly moved to the note. If someone wanted to hurt me, I was sure I had given them ample reason. *If they wanted to hurt Emma...* I let the thought fade away.

When we made it to my home, the air hung thick with her sadness. I placed my hand on the small of her back as I guided her up the dark stairwell. She didn't speak, and I didn't push her. I had no right to ask her what was going on. I excused myself to my room to grab something for her to wear. I needed a moment to think. I raked my hands through my hair trying to figure out what I could do to help her take her mind off what she must be feeling. *I could take away her pain. I could make her forget. But who was going to take my pain away?* I left my room with a new resolve. I wanted her to feel anything but how she felt at this moment. I wanted her to know I was hurting too.

I left my room and made my way toward her.

"I want to show you something." She didn't respond. Her eyes searched my open living room and kitchen. "Come on," I coaxed her. Her eyes fell back to me but not really looking at me. I walked slowly to the other side of the living room. The soft sound of her feet padding behind me on the wood floor was the only sound I could hear over my heartbeat that thudded in my ears.

We reached the elevator doors, and I took a deep breath before opening it. If she ran from me now it would be my undoing. I stepped inside. She hesitated for a brief moment then joined me. We rode silently, side by side, to the floor above.

The doors opened to the large, dark room. I wrapped my arms around her waist and guided her forward, begging her silently not to run. I felt her body tense under my fingertips. I wanted to make her feel at ease. I wanted her to submit herself to me fully so she could forget about the sadness and just feel taken care of.

"What is this?" she asked, her voice stronger than I expected.

"This is where I play."

I felt an involuntary chill run through the length of her body.

Chapter Sixteen

❧

*M*y hand snaked up her body to her throat. I could feel the blood pulsing through the thin skin of her neck as I leaned closer to inhale the scent of flowers wafting from her hair. After everything, I had begun to feel again. I wanted to be with her, to share this with her. My mind thought of her messages and the threat I had received. I was losing my control, and I fucking hated it.

She turned her head slowly to face me, her warm breath blowing across my face.

"I want to hurt you." I had never felt so open, so raw. She didn't run, didn't pull away.

"Maybe I want to be hurt." The words surprised me. I went rigid against her, wondering if I had dreamed it. My body responded, my mouth finding hers. I slipped my hand into her hair and pulled her lips tighter against mine, unable to get enough of her sweet taste. I wanted to drink in as much of her as possible before she realized I was nothing more than a mistake. My own thoughts cut me like a knife.

"Get on your knees," I panted and she obeyed, dropping before me. Her eyes floated up to mine as she waited expectantly. I began undoing my belt, watching her. She didn't move, didn't look away. I unbuttoned my pants and slowly undid the zipper. "Take me in your mouth." My hand slipped back into her long, silky hair. Her hands slid inside my boxers and slowly tugged downward until I was bare in front of her. She gazed at me, unsure of what to do. I wrapped my free hand around myself and pushed forward, the tip of my cock against her warm, parted lips.

Her eyes locked onto mine again as her tongue slowly pushed back against me. I shuddered, unable to keep from showing how badly I wanted her. I rocked my hips again. This time, her lips parted and she let me slide easily inside her warm mouth. Her tongue swirled and circled down my length as I continued to push into her. I licked my lips, wanting to taste her just the same. She began to move faster, her eyes not looking away for even a second. I was completely in control, yet powerless against her. She had done things to me that no other woman had. I craved her. "Stop." The word flew out of my mouth breathy and unsure.

She didn't respond at first. I gripped tighter onto her hair, holding her back. I tugged gently, and she slowly rose to her feet. I couldn't let go, couldn't trust myself to let her go. I took my free hand and slid it down over the curve of her hip, dipping it between the apex of her thighs. Her breath was ragged.

"Please," she begged, and I nearly came at the sound of her voice. I held tightly to her hair, not wanting to give over the only thing I had. Control.

"I like it when you beg." Her chest rose and fell rapidly at my words. I began walking her backward toward the wall, our eyes locked on one another. Her back hit the wall, and she let a small moan escape her lips. I released her hair and grabbed the hem of her shirt, pulling it up roughly over her head. My fingers slowed as I found the button of her jeans and undid them. "You will need a safe word." I leaned in closer, letting her feel my breath across her lips. Her eyes grew wide.

"A safe word?"

"In case you want me to stop." A small hint of a smile ghosted across her face. I knew stopping was the last thing she wanted, but she had no idea what was to come.

"I don't think…" she began. I placed a finger over her lips to keep her from overthinking it.

"It's just in case," I assured her. My breath was ragged, and I didn't know how much longer I could carry on this conversation.

"Flower," she said quickly, her words unsure. I couldn't help but laugh. I had long associated the smell of flowers with her beautiful body.

"Flower," I repeated. My lips met hers, hungrily. Her body responded, pushing against me. Her hands fell to my waist and she began tugging at my undone belt. I grabbed her wrists and pushed her hands above her head. I leaned closer, capturing her bottom lip between my teeth, tugging gently. "Now the real fun begins." I had already broken too many of my rules. I needed to regain my power. I pulled her arms higher, feeling for the metal cuffs above her. I slipped her wrists inside them and tightened them enough to keep her captive.

I pulled back from her reluctantly, wanting to admire the beauty that was her. I dreamed about what she would look like, chained against my wall. It was better than I expected. "You look incredible."

She was mine. I couldn't hide the smile from my face. She was staring at me, waiting. I felt like she could see into the depths of my soul. I pulled a small cloth from my back pocket and stepped back against her. I kissed her softly as I tied the small scrap of fabric over her eyes. I pulled away, wanting to drink her in. I watched as she tugged gently against the restraints, her chest rising and falling heavily.

"William?" My name rolled off her tongue like silk. I broke myself from my trance and leaned in close enough that I knew she felt my body heat.

"Patience," I whispered in her ear, her body arching at my words. I ran my fingers lightly down the inside of her thigh. She quivered under my touch. When I reached her ankle, I tugged on it gently, pulling her legs wider. I grabbed a shackle attached to the floor and secured it around her. I did the same to her other leg. I took my time running the tips of my fingers back up the inside of her legs, stopping at the apex of her thighs.

"This belongs to me now." She was damp against me, and I used her slickness to ease my fingers inside of her. She was panting. "Tell me that you belong to me." Her breathing grew more ragged, but she didn't answer. "Tell me!" I hissed, my jaw clenched.

"I belong to you," she moaned, her hips pulling down toward my fingers. I laughed quietly to myself, wondering what I had done to deserve her.

"Good girl," I breathed into her neck as I trailed kisses down her collarbone. I moved lower, her back arched as I reached her chest. I circled her nipple with my tongue, then lightly bit with my teeth. She cried out, struggling to free herself. I waited, hoping not to hear her utter the safe word. She didn't say anything, and I continued to kiss my way down her stomach, gripping her hips tightly in my hands. I reached to the small shelf beside me and grabbed one of my favorite toys. I clicked it on, and it began to slowly hum. I placed it lightly against her skin; her head jerked down toward it. I could feel her pulse quicken. I slid it up her stomach and around her breast. Her nipple grew tight and budded against it.

"Have you ever played with one of these before?" I asked. She bit her lip and shook her head no. The thought of being her first in so many ways excited me like nothing else. I trailed it back down her abdomen. Her muscles tightened as it tickled her. I kept my eyes on her face as I let it brush against her wet sex. She pulled down on the restraints, the sensation becoming too much for her. "Shhh," I whispered in her ear, not wanting her to hurt herself. I moved it slowly back and forth. Her hips began to rock, matching my rhythm. I hovered my lips above hers, breathing in her quiet panting. "Do you want me to make you cum?"

Her breathing stopped for a split second. "Yes," she cried, leaning forward. I pulled back, unable to give her any control over the situation. I slid the toy faster, moving it effortlessly in her juices.

"Yes what?" I asked as her body writhed against it.

"Yes, sir." Her moan came out low and breathy. I pulled the toy back, not wanting her to cum so quickly. She opened her mouth to protest, and I slid the toy inside. She pulled back, but her head was against the wall. I pressed my body against hers wanting her to feel what she did to me. Heat radiated from her entrance.

"Deeper," I commanded, pushing against her as I pushed with the toy. She let it slide further inside of her mouth. She took the entire length of it. I slowly pulled back and let it trail down over her heaving chest. She was so eager. As I reached her sex, I let it linger where she needed it most as I pushed against her, slipping myself inside. I wasn't slow or gentle. Her body began to buck as her walls clenched around me, pulling me deeper inside of her.

I pulled the toy away and gripped onto her hips, holding still.

"Don't stop," she begged, unable to catch her breath. I rocked my hips toward her, and she squeezed me tightly, bringing herself down onto me farther.

"Tell me what you want."

"I want you." She was desperate for her release.

"You want me to fuck you?" I asked as I pulled back and thrust into her harshly.

"Yes," she cried out.

"Ask nicely." I skimmed my teeth over the shell of her ear.

"Please." She pushed against me.

"Please what?" I asked, pulling my body back from hers, nearly withdrawing completely. I had to force myself to keep any distance between us.

"Please fuck me."

Her words unraveled me. I pushed back inside of her hard. A low moan escaped her lips, and I growled in response, capturing her lips in mine. I wanted to taste every part of her as she came. Her body jerked and tightened around me. I kept pace, wanting to soak up every drop of her pleasure. I came hard as she pulled me impossibly deep inside of her.

I bent down and unlocked her ankles. She brought them together immediately. *At least if she leaves now she knows what she is missing.* I stood, admiring her beauty for one last moment before pulling the cloth from her eyes. I stared past her as I undid her wrists.

"Thanks," she whispered. I found my jeans and turned my back to her as I pulled them on. I felt empty. I walked toward the elevator, the sound of her feet on the wood floor in the distance. We rode down to the next floor in silence. I was so incredibly selfish. I knew she had doubts about me, but I chased after her. She never had a choice. She was vulnerable and sad, and I knew exactly what to say and do to get my way. I felt ill.

As we reached my living space, she headed straight for the bathroom. I didn't doubt that she wanted to cleanse her body of me. I picked up her phone from the counter and began flipping through the settings absentmindedly. My phone rang, and I dug in my pocket to retrieve it. A small, folded piece of paper came with it. I threw it on the counter and looked at my phone. Angela was the last person I wanted to talk to, but I knew if I ignored her she may just show up. I walked toward my living room, trying to put some more distance between Emma and me.

"What?" I snapped, not caring how she felt.

"What's wrong with you?" she asked, and I didn't know how to respond. There were too many answers to that question.

"Let's start with the note," I hissed, trying to keep my voice low.

"William, I don't know what you're talking about." She sounded confused and hurt. I wasn't going to let her off the hook.

"I'm not the only one who could get hurt if anyone found out about us," I threatened. I heard her suck in a shocked breath.

"William, I swear. I didn't do anything." She was begging me to believe. Emma slowly walked past me to the kitchen. I ran my hands through my hair, wishing I had the strength to keep her out of my fucked up world. I didn't have control anymore.

Whoever had sent me the note made sure of that. I turned my back to Emma and lowered my voice.

"It's not a fucking joke. If you did this, I will find out." I hung up, not wanting to hear any more of her excuses. If it wasn't her, then I had much bigger problems on my hands. I walked to the fridge, yanking it open to grab a beer.

"What's wrong?" Emma asked.

So naive. My world was unraveling around me, and I was going to take her down with me. I was a monster. I slammed the fridge and took the top off the bottle. She stared at me expectantly.

"This is what's wrong. This is why I came to see you this morning." I shoved my finger at the note and waited for her to say something, anything. Her eyes danced over the scrap of paper.

"What does this have to do with me?" she asked, confusion twisting her face. "It was that woman wasn't it? The one I saw you with at the theater." She looked back at me, not able to hide the hurt from her eyes. "We have to call the police!"

I shook my head and took another drink from my beer. There had to be another way out of this.

"It's not that simple." Did she not understand that if the police began digging around, it would ruin her life?

"What are you talking about? She threatened your life!" she was shouting. This was a side of her I had never seen before. *She is worried about me. Maybe she is worried about herself.* I took another drink as I thought that over.

"She doesn't seem to know anything about you," I reassured her. She looked confused at my words, running her hands through her knotted hair.

"Shit," she muttered, trying to free her fingers. I smiled and pulled open a drawer on the island and pulled out a pink hairbrush, a reminder of Abby. My thoughts never went to her.

"We have to find somewhere safe for you to go tonight." My stomach panged at the thought of her leaving, but I knew it was best for her.

"Why can't I stay here?" she asked as she brushed the last few tangles from her hair. *She wanted to stay.* "Never mind." She quickly followed, placing the brush on the counter and standing. I had to swallow hard before explaining.

"It's not that I don't want you to stay. I wish I could lock you up and never let you leave." I had to keep the smile from my face. I very much wanted to do that. "The last place you should be is with me." The words hurt as they left my lips. I walked around the island and placed my hands on her cheeks, stroking her face with my thumbs. My body lit up with the electricity between us. "Why do you think so little of yourself?" Her eyes grew wide, and she didn't answer for a moment.

"Why are you so distant?" she countered, and I held my breath as all the reasons flashed across my mind.

"That has nothing to do with you, Emma." She kept her eyes locked on mine. Her hand slowly lifted, and she gently touched her fingertips to my chest. I fought the urge to pull away. I took my hand from her face and placed it on top of hers and held it firm against me. My pulse quickened.

"You are the only person who has ever made my heart race like this." I didn't look away. I needed her to know that. It was probably the most honest words I had ever spoken. I took my other hand and tucked her chestnut hair behind her ear. I swallowed hard at the next words I had to say. "You have to go. It's not up for debate." I kept my tone low and commanding. I couldn't stand if she pushed any further. I wouldn't be able to make her go.

Chapter Seventeen

❦

Emma called one of her friends and left a message letting them know that she wanted to hang out. I made quick work of fixing us something to eat. I made spaghetti as she watched me, not saying a word. We ate together in silence for what felt like an eternity. The thought of her leaving weighed heavy on my heart. Emma was the first to break the silence.

"This is amazing," she said as she slurped up a long noodle. I couldn't help but laugh. I took the pad of my thumb and wiped away some sauce that had collected at the corner of her mouth. Without thinking, I licked my finger. A surprisingly intimate act. She stared at me, and I felt myself go weak under her gaze.

"Eat," I said with a smile, letting my mind forget about everything else. Her phone rang, breaking me from my daydream. She reached for it, tearing her gaze from mine.

"It's Becka," she said before answering it. I grabbed our plates and took them over to the sink, cursing myself for letting someone in.

"My aunt and I had a fight. I just…can't go back there for a while." My heart sank as I listened to her words. I knew that she was lying about her reason, but there was truth in what she was saying as well. "Thanks, Becka. I really appreciate it." She set her phone back on the counter while I finished rinsing off our plates. "She said I could stay." Her words cut through me. I didn't want her to go, but I knew she needed to be as far away from me as possible. I was no good for her, no good for anybody. I shut off the water and turned to face her. I grabbed her purse from the counter and opened the door, waiting for her to follow.

"You can call me if you need anything," I said as we made our way to my car. I wanted her to call me. I wanted to hear her voice again, but this was starting to feel like good-bye. I opened her door for her and waited for her to slip in. To my surprise, she kissed me gently on the cheek, letting her mouth linger. She should hate me. I was the reason she hurt. I couldn't stop myself. I needed to feel her. I turned my head and captured her mouth with mine. Her body relaxed against mine, fitting perfectly against me. I pulled back, cursing myself as I did.

"We have to go." She leaned toward me again but stopped herself. Good. She finally understood that I was the cause of all of this. "I will fix this." I didn't say all of the other things that I wanted to. That fixing this meant I probably would never see her again. She nodded and lowered herself into the seat. I sighed and closed her door.

We rode quietly to her friend's house. The GPS gave directions over the low, muffled sounds of Kings of Leon on the radio. We pulled over just down the street from her friend's house. "I'll come for you as soon as I can," I said, not sure if she heard my voice waver. She had no idea how hard I would struggle to stay away from her. I smiled weakly at her, trying to reassure her.

"I know," she said quietly as she got out of the car. A lump had formed in my throat, and I was unable to say anything else. She stood there, watching me. I fixed my eyes on the road and left, staring at her through the rearview mirror until I couldn't see her any longer.

I ran my hand through my hair and hit the steering wheel, causing the car to swerve slightly into the other lane. "Fuck!" I had lost control. I was dangerously close to folding like a house of cards perched precariously on the ledge of a cliff. Brought down by an innocent. I laughed at the irony of it all. I had messed around with some of the most conniving and manipulating women on the planet, but Emma brought me to my knees. What does she get in return? I put her life in danger.

I turned my car toward the one place I knew could give me comfort. A place that I could torture myself without being judged. A place that I could be tortured by others.

I turned on the next road and sped across town to the run-down and seemingly abandoned strip mall. I stopped first at a gas station along the way and bought a large bottle of bourbon. As I pulled into the parking lot and made my way to the back of the building, I had thoughts of her. She would be laughing and having fun with her friend. She would be thinking of me, of us. I opened the bottle and took a long swig. I stared at the back of the building trying to think of anything else, anyone else. I took another long drink. My veins began to warm as the alcohol swam through me. I grabbed my phone and began typing. I wanted her to push me over the ledge, get it over with.

Chapter Eighteen

Do you have any idea what I want to do to you right now?
I sent the text and took another long drink from the bottle. A few seconds later, my phone vibrated.

Who is this? It is so hard to keep my admirers straight.

My eyes narrowed at the phone. I knew she was joking, but she had no idea how those words ripped through me. That was it; that was the push I needed.

Not funny. I can think of a few ways to punish you later.

I hit send and tossed the phone on the seat next to me. I drank again and closed the bottle before getting out of my car.

The building was quiet, and no one from the outside knew what went on behind these walls. A place like this required an invitation. I had found it after I met a woman at a bar not far from here. She made me realize what I needed.

I stepped into the dark building, eying the women who sat on their knees waiting for someone to come and sweep them off their feet. My gaze fell on J, the receptionist who always greeted me with a warm smile. It was a small crime, and I had no excuse.

"Good evening, sir," she chimed like a bell. I gave her a quick smile, not wanting to make small talk. The alcohol possessed me now, and I just wanted to be numb. "The usual?" Her lips curved into a wicked grin. I nodded and turned to make my way back through the narrow hall. "Sir?" She called after me. I paused, turning back to face her. "If you're up for something different…" her voice trailed off.

She motioned to the girls who sat waiting patiently. "Or perhaps…" She bit her lip as she traced the line of her cleavage with her finger, dipping below the neckline of her already low-cut blouse. I turned away and continued down the hall. I placed my hand on the doorknob of room three and took a minute to steady myself. I had drunk more than I realized, and it was hitting me harder than expected. I stepped inside and removed my shirt, kicking off my shoes at the same time. I stumbled, but managed to keep my balance as I finished getting ready. The door creaked and I sunk to my knees, the weight of the world holding me down. The sound of high heels clicked across the hard floor.

"I didn't expect to see you so soon," she said as she walked around me. I didn't look up. All I could see were her feet in impossibly high heels and her black stockings. "Needing another lesson?" There was amusement in her voice, and it irritated the fuck out of me. She bent closer to me from behind, her hot breath on my ear.

"Maybe today I teach you some discipline," she purred. My lip twitched. Her hand pulled lazily over my shoulder as she rounded in front of me. "Maybe today I teach you pain." Her fingertips were on my chin, angling me up to look at her. My hand shot out and grabbed her wrist before I could think about what I was doing.

"I have more pain than you could give," I said through gritted teeth. Her eyes held wide in shock as I forced her to look deep into mine. I held her tightly as I rose to my feet. She sunk lower until her knees touched the floor, rocking back until she rested on her heels. I stood over her, her wrist tight in my grip. After a moment of silence she spoke.

"Yes, Master." The words sent a chill through my body. I released her and grabbed my clothes, pulling them on quickly.

I made my way out of the building, not making eye contact with anyone as I went. I doubled over, resting my hands on my knees as I reached the cold night air. I wanted to vomit; I was so disgusted with myself. I staggered back to my car and climbed inside, grabbing the bottle of alcohol. I took a long swig and waited for the burning to pass before picking up my phone.

Looking forward to it.

The text I had not waited to see from Emma flashed on the screen. She deserved better. I took another drink before typing out my reply.

You will be sorry you said that.

I knew she wouldn't take it as the warning I had intended. I wasn't strong enough to push her away. I took another drink, glancing at the half-filled bottle. I let my head fall back on the seat as I cranked the engine and let myself get lost in the music.

"I want to take my love and hate you till the end" rang through the speakers. I closed my eyes, slipping deeper into my sadness. My phone beeped and I was almost afraid to pick it up.

I miss you.

I repeated the words over and over again in my head. *What would she think of me now?* I was sick.

Emma, don't.

I hit send and hoped that she would be mad. I couldn't stand her feeling anything like that, but she needed to. She needed to hate me.

Chapter Nineteen

❧

I sat alone, bottle in hand, as I listened to one depressing song after another. The walls I had built to keep everyone out were crumbling around me. I could no longer numb the pain I felt with alcohol or a one-night stand. I had no choice but to face it head-on.

As I sat, lost in my self-induced pain, my phone glowed to life. I had enabled the tracking on Emma's phone, purely for her safety. At least that is the lie I told myself. Regardless of my excuses, she was leaving the safety of her friend's home and making her way to the busier side of town. I growled as my anger began to boil over. I had sent her away for her own safety, and she was already putting herself in more danger. Didn't she know the kind of men that were out at this time of night? Men who wanted to take advantage of her. Men like me. Does she have no sense of self-preservation at all?

I pulled out of the parking lot and followed the small glowing dot. She was unknowingly moving closer to me. It only took me a moment to spot the small cherry red convertible. I slipped inside the club and made my way to the far side of the bar. It took every ounce of my willpower not to go to her side.

She was surrounded by men, and with the clothes that she was wearing, it wasn't a surprise. I watched her, trying to convince myself that she wasn't mine to worry about, but the note had made that decision for me. She was in danger, whether she took that seriously or not, but I had to. I pulled out my phone and dialed her number.

"Bad girl," I said, and I heard her breathe heavily into the phone.

"We just went out for a few drinks. How did you…" Her voice trailed off. She nervously bit down on her bottom lip.

"Stop biting your lip before I bend you over the bar and punish you right here." I couldn't help but laugh at my own twisted thoughts. I lie to myself about protecting her, and all the while I want to torture her. I stared past the pretty little blond who had perched herself between us. I waited. Emma's gaze scanned the bar until it finally fell on me. Her cheeks burned with anger. I knew she would be upset that I was here. I didn't care.

"How did you know?" Her face looked like she was trying to solve a problem in her head. I smiled.

"I activated the GPS on your phone." I motioned for the bartender to fill my drink, knowing I was going to need it.

"You what?" She was angry. Over her shoulder, Becka had noticed me, and I heard her say my name in the receiver. I turned quickly, trying to make it less obvious whom I was staring at.

"We are leaving now." I wanted to take her back to my place. It would be safer than this club.

"I'll be out for a few more hours," she replied, and the phone went dead. *How could she not understand that I was trying to protect her?* I glared down the bar at her. Becka was hugging her, and over the music I could hear her ordering another round of drinks. I clenched my jaw as I resisted the urge to grab her and carry her out of this place. I sent her a quick message before ordering another drink.

Last chance.

I watched her look down at the phone and shrug before turning away. My stomach knotted. A man came up behind her and wrapped his arms around her waist. I nearly broke the glass in my hand. His name was Jeff Baker, and he was in one of my classes. She looked over her shoulder, smiling. Pain ripped through me as I watched her exchange pleasantries with him. His hands lingered on her body. I typed out a quick warning, hoping she would end this little game.

I will fucking kill him if he puts his hands on you again.

I didn't know how seriously she would take my threat, but I meant every word. She didn't look my way. Hand in hand, she and her new friend walked out onto the dance floor and began to move against one another. His hands moved possessively over her body. I felt the heat in my body rise as I thought how I would make him pay.

"You wanna dance?" The pretty little blond was leaning closer, and I finally allowed myself to look at her. She smiled and ran her fingers down my chest. I grabbed her wrist and pulled it back from my body. She looked rejected. I pulled her toward me so her face was inches from mine. *I wonder what Emma will think. I wonder if she would feel the way I feel with someone else touching her.* The blond stepped closer, filling the void between us.

"You seem like a man who knows what he wants," she whispered in my ear.

Emma turned around and our eyes met for a brief moment.

"It's not you. I'm sorry," I whispered back in her ear. Emma had already resumed her dance. I pushed the blond away from me slightly so I could slide out from behind her. She stormed off, rejected. I knew exactly how she felt. I made my way outside, letting the cool night air pull me away from the thudding beat of the music and the equally fast beat of my heart. I stumbled to my car, looking for refuge. I couldn't leave her here, not knowing how she will get home and if she will be safe. If she will be alone.

I sat for a few minutes doing a little searching on my phone to find out more about Jeff while I waited. It only took a minute to locate him as a newly added friend on one of Emma's social network pages. I read over his information, looked through his pictures. It is amazing how much personal information people willingly give out without a second thought. I thought of how easy it would be for whoever threatened me to find out the same from Emma. Within minutes, you could find out where someone lived and where and whom they liked to hang out with. A flood of light came from the front of the building, catching my attention.

Emma stepped out of it like an angel exiting the gates of heaven. She was looking at her phone, oblivious to my presence. I waited, hoping no one would follow her out. No one did. The doors closed slowly behind her as she made her way out to the street and began walking toward her home with no concern for the dangers that lurked in the darkness.

I felt the anger rise inside of me again. I pulled out behind her. She didn't look at me as I pulled up beside her, and it ripped me apart inside.

"Get the fuck in the car." I didn't care how it sounded. All I cared about was her safety. She stopped but still didn't look my way. "Don't make me repeat myself," I warned, hoping she knew just how serious I was. She bit down on her lip and got in, not looking my way. I drove off into the night, wanting to put as much distance between us and the club as possible. She was killing me inside, and she was oblivious to it, or she just didn't care. The thought made my anger magnify. We drove in silence. The only sound was the clicking of her seat belt as we sped down the dark road.

I pulled inside the garage bay of my building, not waiting for the door to close completely behind us before getting out and slamming the door hard. I couldn't think straight, couldn't guarantee her safety with me. I ran my hands through my hair and made my way up to the next floor, not waiting for her.

I waited at the top of the stairs as I counted every step she took, closing the gap of space between us. She looked down at the ground as she walked by and made her way inside. How fitting it was to watch her only moments before walking out of the light, and now she followed me into the darkness.

Chapter Twenty

❧

I walked inside, locking the door behind me. I didn't say a word, didn't look her way. I walked to the far side of the room to the elevator and waited for the doors to open. I wanted to take her for granted. I listened, counting the steps she took across the hardwood floor before taking her place by my side.

The ride to the next level was excruciatingly long. She didn't look my way, didn't make any attempt to touch me. As the doors opened, again I stepped out onto the dark floor.

"Come here," I said, looking back at her. She hesitated but stepped forward.

"What are you thinking?" she asked. She wanted to sound confident, but her voice betrayed her, wavering under her words. I smiled as I thought of how many answers there were to that question.

"I was thinking…I don't know if I can trust myself with you right now." I glanced at her, gauging her reaction.

I wouldn't have blamed her if she fled. If she knew anything about me, she knew I was to be taken seriously. I wanted to hurt her. I always wanted to hurt her for the way she made me feel. I didn't want to feel at all. I didn't want to be hurt again. More than anything, I didn't want her to have to feel any of that pain. It was torture and after her display tonight, I couldn't help but think she enjoyed inflicting me with it. She was biting her lip and staring at me. Not running, not looking at me with disgust. I reached over and used my thumb to free her lip from her teeth.

"I trust you." Her words came out stronger, and her voice was steady. I knew she meant it. The thought made me sick. I was leading the wounded doe-eyed deer to slaughter, and she willingly came.

"You wouldn't say that if you had any idea what I thought about doing to you tonight." I was being brutally honest with her. She stepped toward me, and every muscle in my body stiffened. She had no sense of self-preservation. I had no willpower to stay away from her.

"Punish me," her voice barely above a whisper. My eyes shot to hers as I searched them. "Punish me," she repeated. She slowly reached toward me, her fingertips trailing down my chest and over my stomach. I glanced down at her fingers and back to her.

"Do you remember the safe word?" I asked, wanting her to understand what kind of events I had planned for her. She swallowed hard.

"Flower," she whispered. I grabbed her wrists tightly, not able to stay away any longer. I pulled her across the room. My eyes scanned the room, trying to decide exactly how I wanted to punish her. I came to a stop in front of one of my favorite devices. It had a large incline on one side and two smaller on the other.

"Bend over." I couldn't look her in the eye. Not with the thoughts I had running through my head. She stared at me helplessly, unsure of what she should do. I spun her around and pushed her down over the device, her body folding over the top of it. I sunk to my knees and secured her ankles in the leather straps on each incline. I wasn't wasting my time making it sensual. I came around to the other side of her and pulled her arms toward the floor, securing them as well. She looked up at me helplessly, but I didn't meet her gaze.

"William, I'm sorry." She was on the verge of tears. That only made me angrier.

"Not nearly as sorry as you are going to be." I moved back behind her, not wanting her eyes on me any longer. She could see past my walls I had built up. It scared me. I pulled my belt from my pants and wasted no time making her feel the pain I had all night. I came down across her backside, and she pulled against the restraints. I waited but no safe word came. I struck again. She didn't scream, barely letting a whimper escape. I struck again, not bothering to soothe her or comfort her. Again. Again. My adrenaline was coursing through my body, and I was on a different plane of existence. Again. Again.

"Stop!" She cried out. I struck again. Again. "Please," she cried out, louder this time. She didn't say the safe word, and I didn't slow.

"Do you have any idea what I wanted to do to you at that club? Any idea what I wanted to do to that guy who had his hands all over you?" I struck again, carefully hitting a different spot than the last.

"I'm sorry." Her words were choked. "Please." I could hear the crying in her words. I let the belt slip between my fingers; it banged loudly on the hardwood floor, echoing around us. I had hurt her. I quickly undid her leg restraints and made my way to the front of her to undo her wrists. Her head hung in defeat in front of me. I tipped her chin up, angling her face toward mine. I wiped her swollen tear-stained cheeks with my finger and quickly lifted her in my arms. I carried her to the elevator, wanting to get her as far away from this place as possible. She buried her face in my neck and began to sob quietly.

"Why didn't you use the safe word?" I asked as her eyes met mine. I felt my gut wrench at the sight of her in so much pain.

"I didn't want to upset you." She nuzzled back against me. I was sickened by her confession. Until this moment, I thought she didn't care. *How could she care?* Now she was putting herself in danger to please me. *Animal.*

I carried her to my bathroom. I set her down, making sure she was steady on her feet before running the water.

"What are you doing?"

I didn't know how to respond. I wanted her to wash away any lingering of me. I wanted to make her whole again. Pure.

"I thought a bath might make you feel better." She looked at me dazed for a moment before stumbling forward and placing her hand on my chest. I didn't pull away. I deserved any discomfort or pain she could inflict upon me.

"Please don't go." Her voice was full of sadness. A lone tear slid down her pink cheek. I wiped it away, wishing it were that easy to get rid of all of her pain. She pushed forward, her mouth finding mine, hungrily. I couldn't resist her. For a moment, I gave in. She slipped her tongue past mine. I pulled back, wishing I hadn't ever acted on my feelings for her.

"Get washed up. You will feel better." I turned off my emotions, not wanting to feel anything anymore. I left, closing the door behind me, hearing her muffled sobs in the back of my mind.

I had ruined her life in the short time I had known her. I lied to myself, telling myself I was helping her, protecting her. The only person she needed protection from was me. I couldn't control myself when I was around her. My every waking thought was clouded and consumed by her.

I made my way into my bedroom. Sinking down on the edge of my bed, I ran my hands through my hair. I needed to protect her from me. I needed to right all of the wrongs I had done. I grabbed my phone and called an old friend—one of the very few people I considered that.

"I need you to do me a favor." I didn't waste my time with pleasantries. If I was calling, he knew it was serious.

"Jesus Christ, William. What did you get yourself into now?" Stephen asked, laughing to himself. Stephen and I were old college buddies. I helped him out of a few situations, and he still owed me.

"I need you to do a little digging for me." I explained the situation with the note and Emma and all of the shit I had gotten her into. He sighed and the line hung silent for a few minutes.

"I'll see what I can find out about this Jeff and get back to you. William, are you sure..." His voice quieted and he didn't have to finish his sentence for me to know exactly whom he was talking about.

"I'm sure," I said, not wanting even to entertain the thought of her with someone else. The door let out a loud creak behind me. I spun around to see Emma wearing nothing. "Call me back if you hear anything. I have to go." I couldn't help but stare at her. She was absolute perfection.

"Emma," I sighed, hoping she would turn and run from me. I walked slowly toward her, stopping a few steps away.

"Are you mad at me?" she asked, and a sadistic laugh escaped me.

"How could I ever be mad at you?" I knew I should have made myself stop. I should have blown her off for her own good, but I was drawn to her. I stepped forward, kissing her lightly on the forehead. "I'm mad at myself." I deserved the pain I was putting myself though. "Get dressed. I'll take you home." I forced myself to step back from her. I turned to my dresser and pulled out a T-shirt and a pair of my jeans for her to wear.

"But… you said it wasn't safe for me there." She took the clothing and held it over her body. I wasn't strong enough to push her away.

"It's not safe for you with me." It hurt to say it, but she needed to understand. She took a step toward me, and I had to put up a hand to stop her. If she came any closer, I would lose myself. I wanted to have her in every way possible, to possess her. She didn't move and I couldn't help the disappointment that crept over me. I ran my hands through my hair, frustrated.

"You can have the bed; I'll take the couch." I walked out of the room, forcing myself to leave her there alone. I pushed the thought of slamming her against the wall and fucking her the way she wanted me to. My cock throbbed at the idea. I went to the bathroom and splashed cold water on my face. On the way back to the couch, I had to force myself not to go to her.

I lay awake for hours, thinking of her. Thinking of her naked body wrapped in my sheets. Thinking of my hands roaming over her soft skin. Then I thought about Jeff's hands on her body at the club. Rage boiled inside of me.

I could hear her tossing and turning. I told myself I needed to make sure she was OK. I walked over to the door that sat ajar and peered inside. She tossed and turned, tangling herself in the sheets. Her face looked in pain, but her body writhed like she was in the midst of passion. I grew hard. Her eyes flew open and locked onto mine as she bit down on her lip.

"It was just a nightmare," she said, struggling to steady her breathing. If it was a nightmare, I knew it involved me. I walked out of the room without saying a word.

I walked to the kitchen and grabbed my phone. I sent Stephen a quick text to see if he found anything out. I poured a drink while I waited, staring at my bedroom door. There was no sound; I was certain she had drifted back off to sleep. My phone lit up.

Nothing serious. He did have a complaint filed against him last year. Seems he got a little aggressive with a female, but nothing ever came of it.

I swallowed hard, trying to stop the bile that rose in my throat. I took another long drink and grabbed my keys. I did warn her that I would kill him if he touched her again.

As I made my way to the club, I scanned the parking lot to see who was still around. I recognized Jeff's car from his online pictures. Amazing how much information we give away online. I checked my watch. The club was less than an hour from closing. I parked a few spaces away and made my way over to his vehicle. I wanted to wait for him. I wanted to look him in the eye when I hurt him for touching her. I couldn't risk it. If anyone knew about us, she would never be able to escape it. To escape me.

I tried the driver's side door. Locked. I moved back, looking around to make sure no one was around. I was alone. I pulled the handle, and the door swung open. I smiled at how easy he made it. I reached up and unlocked the front door, sliding inside. I popped the hood and walked to the front of the car. I took one last look around before reaching in and loosening the brake line.

I slipped back inside the house quietly, hoping she hadn't awakened while I was gone.

Chapter Twenty-One

I stood in the kitchen in my boxers waiting for the coffee to brew. I was nervous to know if she awoke last night to find me gone. I forced myself not to turn on the news to see if Jeff had been involved in a horrible drunk driving accident. Tragic as that would be, I felt no pity for him. If she had seen the look in his eyes when he touched her. The same look mirrored in my eyes thousands of times before, I'm sure.

I heard her stir a few minutes later, and I busied myself, pouring the coffee. I turned to face her as I heard her draw near. I ran my hand through my hair, trying to push the thought of how lovely she looked in my oversized shirt and nothing else. She looked to the ground and tucked her hair behind her ear.

"Coffee smells good," she said, breaking the spell. I handed her a cup of coffee and quickly drank mine, pouring another cup.

"Didn't sleep?" she asked, not accusingly.

"I had a lot on my mind." My eyes danced over her.

"I'm sorry about everything last night." She looked sad and guilty. I wondered if I looked guilty.

"I hurt you, and you apologize." I laughed at the irony. "Emma, I am no good for you. I knew what I was doing the first moment I saw you. I should have stopped it. I shouldn't have let it go this far."

"I wanted you just as badly as you wanted me," she said quietly. She didn't get it. She didn't understand how dangerous I was for her. For all I knew, I killed someone last night because he had touched her. I slammed my hands down on the counter between us. She jumped at the loud noise.

"I scare you. Good. Maybe now you will stay away from me." The words burned my throat as I said them. I couldn't imagine never touching her again. Not being there to protect her. But who would protect her from me?

"You don't mean that." She stepped around the island, closing the distance between us.

"It's for your own good, Emma." I wanted her, for once in her life, to think about her own safety. She stopped, not stepping any closer. Her eyes looked through me as she searched for any truth in my words. Without saying another word, she turned and made her way to the bathroom. Her steps were faster than I would have liked. She was sad. I wanted to run to her, to hold her. I didn't.

Instead, I went to my room and got dressed. When I returned the air was thick with regret. When Emma exited the bathroom, she was wearing her clubbing clothes. I knew she had finally understood. I had finally been able to push her away.

We didn't speak. I grabbed my keys, and she followed behind me to my car. I opened the door and watched her slide inside.

She winced as her bottom touched the seat and angled herself away from me.

"Emma," I sighed.

"Don't," she cut me off. I couldn't blame her. I didn't try to talk to her again. It was sick of me to constantly push her away only to pull her back for my own selfish needs.

The trip to the grocery store where her car was parked seemed especially short. The instant I put the car in park, she opened her door and slammed it behind her. I didn't deserve anything more. I knew that.

"Emma," I called after her, trying to convince myself that I had to make sure she was OK. She ignored me, digging through her purse for her keys. The bag fell from her grasp, spilling its contents all over the ground. "Shit, Emma." I got out and rushed to her side, helping her collect her things. "I'm just trying to protect you." I was growing frustrated with her. *Why couldn't she just fucking understand I am trying to protect her?* Tears began to roll down her face. *Fuck.* I wiped her tears away with the back of my hand. I let my thumb slip across her lower lip. *God, she was so fuckable even when she was sad.*

"By hurting me?" she asked, her chin trembling.

"I didn't mean to hurt you. You didn't use the safe word." I regretted the words as they left my mouth. Had I really just blamed her? She didn't know any better. I should have been more cautious. "You deserve better." It was the most honest thing I had said to her.

"What about the note? What if someone comes looking for me?" I wasn't a stranger to women trying to manipulate me, and I knew that was exactly what she was trying to do. I also knew she was right. Someone could come looking for her. I wouldn't let that happen.

"I will take care of that today." I hoped she knew I meant it. She would always be safe as long as she stayed away from me. She didn't respond. Maybe she did understand. She got in her car and drove off. I waited, thinking about how I would make all of this right.

Chapter Twenty-Two

I drove back to my house feeling empty. Every second I spent without her felt like an eternity. I hated how weak and out of control I had become. I was risking myself, doing things without hesitation or planning. Like what I did to Jeff. As much as I wanted to make myself feel guilty, I couldn't. The emotion just wouldn't come. I told myself I was protecting her. No one was protecting her from me.

As soon as I got home, I stripped off my clothes and took a cold shower. I let the water wash over me as if it could wash away my sins. The ocean didn't even hold enough water for that. I washed myself as if it could, scrubbing harder than necessary until my skin burned like fire against the soap. It still wasn't enough. The pain paled in comparison to the pain I had caused her. To the pain I would cause her. I let my hand lower, stroking myself at the thought of her. She was so innocent, so trusting. I never gave her a reason to trust me, but she did. I squeezed tighter, allowing a twinge of pleasure to ripple through my body before stopping myself. I didn't deserve any kind of release. I cocked back my fist and struck the wall allowing myself, instead, the pain that I deserved.

It pumped through me, throbbing up my arm into my chest. It felt good. It felt real. It felt deserved.

I let the water run ice cold before getting out and drying myself off. I switched on the television as I dipped inside my bedroom for clean clothes. I came back out to the sound of the news. They had just finished a story about a drunk driving accident in the early morning hours. I smiled, but it was short-lived when they said he was going to be fine. *For now.* They also mentioned a suspicion of foul play, but with his blood alcohol level being what it was, they didn't take it very seriously. Still, I would have to come up with a plan just in case.

I grabbed my phone and sent Angela a message. I needed to meet her face-to-face and put an end to all of this. I wasn't going to let her hurt Emma. I deserved whatever pain was brought upon me, but Emma was innocent. I had manipulated and used her for my own gain.

As I waited for her to get back to me, I searched the Internet to arrange for after graduation. I knew I wouldn't be able to take Emma away before the end of the year without telling her the truth about Jeff. I would just have to risk it and hope for the best. If anything were to happen before then, I would just have to do whatever it took to make her safe—whatever that may be.

I was exhausted. I spent the entire night thinking of her. Even when I did manage to fall asleep from sheer exhaustion, her face haunted my dreams. I could smell her, taste her on my lips. She was an addiction that I didn't want cured. The utterance of her name caused my body to go rigged and my cock to grow hard. Her twisted sense of self and lack of any kind of discipline only made me crave her that much more.

I made my way to work, hoping I would get a chance to see Emma. I waited anxiously for her to come. I needed another fix. I grabbed her books and placed them on her desk. It felt like an eternity since I had looked in her eyes—since I had broken her heart and pushed her away. I leaned against my desk, my blood pounding in my ears as my heart raced. As she walked through the door, her eyes caught mine and for a second the world stood still and spun faster at the same time, spiraling out of control and orbiting around us. The high was short-lived as one of my students came to ask me a question about our last assignment. I answered him quickly and turned back to her, but she had disappeared. Like a beautiful mirage. My eyes scanned the room frantically before coming to rest on her.

She held a smile on her face but didn't look at me. I struggled to regain my composure and begin the lesson. I prepared questions to engage the class and to keep myself from fantasizing about her. I asked a few questions, all the while glancing in her direction. She continued to avoid my gaze and appeared not even to be listening.

"Emma... Emma!" I called out, breaking her from her daydream. She looked embarrassed as her eyes shot up and the class looked at her expectantly.

"What?" she asked, not bothering to hide her irritation with me.

I deserved it, but I didn't like it. I bit back the urge to scold her, to tell her she needed to be punished. I had no right to say anything to her at all.

"Who exacted punishment on the rebels of the North of England referred to as 'The Harrying of the North'?" I stared at her, not letting her look away from me. I wanted her to hear the word punishment and think of me. As her cheeks burned pink, I knew that she had. Her brain searched for an answer—an answer that I knew she didn't have, since I had her book all weekend. If she thought of me, of punishment, she could put two and two together. Her eyes lit up as she did just that.

"William the Conqueror?" she responded with a smirk. I had used William the Conqueror as my contact name when I programmed my number into her phone.

"That is correct, Ms. Townsend." I bit back a grin. "Good girl." I made sure her eyes were locked onto mine as I said it. I knew what those words would do to her. She bit her lip as she flushed. I narrowed my eyes at her, staring at her mouth. *Her pretty fuckable mouth.* She released her lip immediately.

I broke away from her and continued to ask questions. My thoughts never left her, though. I ran my hand over the edge of the desk where her fingers had gripped, holding it tightly while I punished her. I ran my hand over the buckle of my belt, which awarded me another lusty stare. My cock twitched and I had to discreetly adjust myself.

Time switched into hyper-speed, and before I knew it, the class was emptying. I fought the urge to ask her to stay, knowing if I asked she would. She would want to please me. I licked my lips and glanced up in time to see her glance over her shoulder. She looked sad. I knew I was the cause of it.

I thought of nothing else for the rest of the day. I wanted to take away her pain—the pain I had given her.

I made my way to my car and waited for her to come out. She made small talk with her friends before sitting in her car alone. I couldn't resist texting her. I wanted her to know that I was thinking about her.

You are incredibly beautiful, even when you're sad.

She smiled, and I felt my stomach tighten. Her face relaxed again, and she knew that I was watching.

Is that why you broke my heart?

Her words cut through me with gut-wrenching pain.

I would give anything to take back all of the pain I have caused you.

I watched her as a smile played across her lips.

Some of the pain we enjoyed.

She had no idea what she did to me. Reading words alone made me stiff, painfully so. I took a deep breath and fought the urge to take her in her car.

Go home, Emma.

Angela was walking toward my car, and I needed time to be alone with her—to threaten her. I glanced back at Emma who was glaring at me.

Now!

I gave her a stern look but had to focus on Angela. I got out of my car and greeted her, trying not to draw attention to us. Emma flew past us, speeding carelessly through the parking lot. I typed quickly, wishing I could go after her.

Slow down.

She sat at the light, waiting for it to change. I swallowed the hard lump in my throat as I waited. When it did she made sure I understood how upset she was. I cringed as her car lurched dangerously into traffic.

"So…" Angela said, her eyes downcast.

"Why the fuck have you been avoiding my calls?" I was livid. More so at Emma who was self-destructing before my eyes.

"I ha-haven't," Angela replied in a hushed tone, searching the lot for anyone who was listening.

"We need to talk...some other time. For now, I don't want to see you. I don't want to even hear you breathe my name. You will regret it." I lowered my voice so no one would hear, but I made sure it kept its edge. She didn't respond, just nodded while fidgeting with her necklace. She turned and made her way to her car.

Chapter Twenty-Three

I didn't waste a second. I needed to make sure that Emma made it home safely. I drove to her place, making sure no one else was home. Emma's car was not there. I parked up the road and walked behind her house, finding her bedroom window unlocked. I smiled at how careless she really was where her safety was concerned. I slipped inside her window and waited anxiously for her to come. It didn't take long. Within the minute, I heard the sound of the garage door raising and lowering. I listened to her as she went about her business, unaware of what could be lurking around the corner. As she made her way down the hall, I felt my pulse quicken in time with her steps.

The door opened.

"So you enjoy the pain?" I asked.

She was too stunned. She didn't reply. Her eyes locked onto mine as if trying to figure out if I was really there.

"Close the door."

She stepped inside and slid the door shut behind her. She leaned back against it, and her eyes flickered to the window. "If Angela knew about you, she isn't going to say or do anything about it," I told her, trying to ease some of her worry. I wasn't going to let anyone hurt her. *Anyone.* If I was strong enough to stay away, I would. She looked confused.

"She's married. The last thing she wants is for her husband to find out she likes fucking other men," I explained.

Her expression changed to hurt, and I cursed myself for revealing more to her than I intended. She looked at her feet, biting her lip out of nervousness. "She wasn't really my type. I like my women all to myself." I took a step closer to her and lifted her chin with my fingers. "Breathe, Emma."

As if my words were her command, she sucked in a ragged breath. I let my hands glide over her body. I traced her jaw as my other explored her waist. I let it slip lower, caressing her hip. She let out a breathy moan, and I continued on, running my fingers down her thigh and hooking my hand underneath her knee. I pulled it quickly and pressed the length of myself against her. I let my lips ghost across her face to her ear. "I miss the taste of you on my lips."

She relaxed, held there by the pressure of my weight against her. She moaned in my ear. I nearly lost myself at the sound. I let my thumb glide over her bottom lip as she parted them. I pushed my finger inside, and she welcomed it with her tongue. "I should go."

"No." Her tone was panicked and full of longing.

"I tried to stay away from you, Emma, but I can't. You consume my every thought. After graduation we should get away from here for a while." She looked hesitant.

I pressed my forehead against hers, inhaling her flowery scent.

"Where?" Her voice was quiet.

"Anywhere. It doesn't matter. Just…far away from this place. I want to wake up to your smile." I looked in her eye, wanting to see her happy. She smiled back at me. I was aching for her to agree. "Say yes."

"Yes, sir." She grinned and I pushed my lips against hers, wanting to taste her, to feel her happiness.

"Be a good girl." I knew how those words affected her. I could see it in her eyes. It was also a warning. I knew that I was in too deep with her now. I couldn't resist her pull, couldn't be responsible for what I would do if she ever left me.

I forced myself to leave so her aunt wouldn't catch us. I couldn't risk it when we were so close to being able to be together. I kept busy the rest of the evening, planning for our upcoming getaway and the end of the school year. I felt like I had control again—a feeling I very much missed.

I searched endless sites but always came back to one—Emma's profile. I loved flipping through her pictures. She looked so sad, so broken. I wanted to change that. I wanted to always make her smile, feel happiness, feel pleasure.

That night I fell asleep to her face as I drifted off on the couch. I didn't want to sleep in my bed alone—a feeling that bothered as much as it comforted. I dreamed of her all night. We went away together where no one knew us. She was at my side everywhere I went.

"You are beautiful." Her cheeks turned pink under the praise. "I have something for you." She sat quietly, patiently waiting. I pulled a velvet box out that I had hidden in a drawer and held it out to her, sinking down on my knee. "Open it." She took it in her delicate fingers and slowly opened the hinged top. Her eyes glowed with excitement. "May I?" I asked, taking the box from her hand. She

watched me as I pulled the leather strap from the box and fixed it
around her neck. "Mine." She sat taller.

The next morning all I could think about was seeing her. I couldn't keep myself away anymore. I drove to work earlier than usual, anxious to catch a glimpse of Emma. My heart was racing like a stampede of wild horses.

I spotted her car immediately. She sat inside, her eyes searching around her. I texted her to let her know I was there.

Eager to learn, Ms. Townsend?

A smile spread across her face.

You are a great teacher.

There are so many more things I would like to teach you, Emma.

I watched her get out of her car and make her way into the building. It took every ounce of self-control not to run after her. Instead, I watched her. Watched her fingers glide through her hair. Watched her hips sway gently as she walked. Watched as she disappeared out of sight. My phone beeped and my heart leaped in my throat, but it was not from Emma. It was my father. He was out on location filming a movie and wanted me to check on his property. I swallowed hard and clenched my jaw. That was all my father ever cared about, his things. He never asked how I was. We had an understanding that we would stay out of each other's lives. That was after he made sure I had lost the only thing I had loved a few years ago. I didn't respond. I grabbed my belongings and made my way inside.

My classroom was empty as usual in the morning. I pulled out my laptop and began searching flights to California. Perhaps I could kill two birds with one stone and take Emma out there. It was on the complete opposite side of the country.

A knock came at the door, and I quickly closed my computer.

"Come in!" I shouted. The door slowly opened, and Tracy stepped inside. She was in the same class as Emma. Her hair was golden blond and long. Her skin had a deep tan.

"What can I do for you, Tracy?" She chewed on her lip as she pulled the door closed behind her, an action that got my attention immediately. She stepped closer, closing the distance between us.

"I was wondering if there was something I can do to help improve my grade. Maybe…some extra credit?" Her fingers traced the collar of her shirt. I splayed my hand out on the desk and rubbed the surface. She smiled seductively as she shifted her weight from one foot to the other. I stood and rounded my desk, walking toward her. Her eyes never left mine as her smile grew wider. I didn't stop, walking past her to the door and pulling it open.

"I suggest you study and do your assignments," I said, smiling back politely. She pouted but reluctantly left the room. I slammed the door behind her and leaned back against it, running my hands through my hair roughly. I was used to being hit on. That was nothing new. I just wasn't used to turning someone down.

The rest of the morning went by quickly, and I was soon anxiously awaiting Emma. The students filed in, chatting for a few minutes before taking their seats. Emma was not among them. I closed the door and began the lecture. I glanced toward the door and caught sight of her. She smiled and I knew what she wanted.

"Ms. Townsend, see me after class." Her cheeks burned red. I was glad I had planned something that would not force me to take my mind off her. "Everyone, clear your desks for the chapter quiz." This close to the end of the year the work no longer meant much of anything, but it was important to keep them on their toes. I circled my desk and took a seat, waiting for the papers to make their way to the back row. I sent Emma a quick text.

I know just how to punish you.

I watched as she read over her phone, then her eyes shot up to meet mine. She bit her lip, and I felt my body go rigid as other parts of me reacted.

Slide the phone between your legs and leave it there.

Now.

She hesitated but did as I told her, slipping the phone down between her thighs. I texted again and watched as her eyes grew wide. Her hands gripped the edge of her desk as it vibrated pleasure through her. I couldn't help but grin, slipping my hand under the desk to rub against myself. I hit send again and watched her mouth fall open, her eyes begging me for sweet release. I licked my lips, wanting to taste hers. I sent another and another, pushing harder against myself, as I grew uncomfortably stiff.

A knock came at the door, and her eyes shot to it wildly. I cleared my throat, doing my best not to sound turned on.

"Come in." I adjusted myself to hide my growing arousal and sat up, waiting for the door to open. Nothing could prepare me for the gut-wrenching pain that sunk in the pit of my stomach. "Abby."

I was in disbelief. The woman who had caused all of my pain had just sauntered in as if she owned the world.

"Will," she said coldly. The sound of her voice made me sick. I jumped to my feet and quickly ushered her outside, wanting to get her as far away from Emma as possible. I glanced back over my shoulder. Emma looked pained, as if she knew exactly who this was, but that was not possible. I closed the door behind us and ran my hands through my hair.

"What do you want?" I made sure she understood I was not happy to see her. She smiled slightly.

"How are you?" she asked.

"What the fuck do you care? When have you ever cared?" I shot back, anger coursing through my veins. I wanted to hurt her. I wanted to make her beg me to stop. I wouldn't stop. She swallowed hard and stepped closer. Her fingertips ran over my jaw. I closed my eyes, letting myself enjoy her touch for a brief moment before grabbing her wrist and pulling her away.

"Have you missed me? Missed us at all?" She looked confused. She had no idea how much pain she had caused me. She was possibly more twisted and fucked up than I ever was.

"Why are you really here?" I was crushed by my own words.

She and I both knew why she was really here. The door flew open, and students began to snake their way around us. We stood there silently as they went on with their lives. I was locked in my past, being tortured all over again.

Past and future collided at once as Emma stepped through the door. Her eyes searched mine.

"Emma, we can discuss you being late some other time." I knew I would have to explain everything to her. Abby glanced at her, and then her eyes stayed locked onto mine.

"No. She can stay. I'd like to get to know the woman who is fucking my husband." Abby was harsh and cruel. Not very different from the man I had become. Emma grabbed her stomach as if she had been punched in the gut. I wanted to wrap my arms around her. She stared at me helplessly, silently pleading me to tell her it was all a lie. "Oh, she didn't know?" Abby said with a laugh. I focused on her throat. I wanted to strangle the laugh out of her.

"Go," I snapped, gesturing for them to get back into the classroom. I glanced down the hall to make sure no one had seen the exchange. There couldn't be any witnesses, just in case we all didn't leave the room. Emma's eyes shot to mine, pained. I hated myself in that moment. They both made their way back inside and waited for me.

"I'm not here to ruin your fun, Will. I just came to get what is mine," she explained, leaning back against my desk. I grabbed my belt, wanting to bend her over it and plead with me to forgive her.

"I don't owe you anything." I struggled to keep my voice low so no one would become alarmed.

"I'm sorry. Did you say you are his wife?" Emma's voice shook.

"Ex-wife," I replied before Abby could open her mouth. She nodded slowly, but I could tell she was having trouble processing the new information. Only moments ago she was on the verge of ecstasy; now her heart was being crushed. Abby's eyes burned into me. I had to clench my fists to keep from reacting. Abby, once one of the most beautiful women in the world in my eyes, now looked like a snarling animal. She was made ugly by greed.

"You really want your little secret getting out?" Her eyes danced between us. "Imagine what the other professors would say. Imagine…what your father would say." She was as sick and twisted as she had been back then. She didn't care about me or my happiness. I didn't care about myself, but I would not let her hurt Emma.

"What is it that you want?" Emma struggled to sound more confident. Abby grinned at her but turned back to me.

"You know what I want, but since that isn't going to happen, a couple million oughta cover it. Don't you think, Will?" Her smile grew wide, but her eyes were dead.

"Where the hell is he going to get money like that?" Emma shot back, not letting Abby ignore her presence.

"Fine," I replied, narrowing my eyes. Abby straightened, feeling as though she had won. "Then you get the fuck out of my life. I don't ever want to see you again."

"You have my number." She winked at me, but it was for Emma to see. She shoved between us and left.

I glanced at Emma, her eyes wide in shock. I stepped closer to her, but she held up her hand in front of me.

"Don't," she said. The word was like nails on a chalkboard. I struggled not to bend her over.

"It was a long time ago."

"How long? You're just out of college and she...how old is she?" A million more questions lurked behind her eyes.

"She was my math teacher in high school."

"And you...you married her?" Even her sadness...beautiful. I stepped closer to her.

"I loved her," I confessed. I knew back then how to feel. That is why Abby was able to hurt me so badly. Emma looked like she was ready to collapse under the weight of my secrets. She leaned back on the desk behind her for support, then pushed herself past me. I grabbed her arm, stopping her.

"I need to get out of here." Her eyes were watery, and I knew she was using all of her strength not to let me see how hurt she was.

"I'll go with you." I searched her eyes for a moment before releasing her arm. I had to make sure she understood. I couldn't lose her. I wouldn't lose her. I grabbed my things and went out to the parking lot to wait for her. No one could see us leave together.

As she came through the door, I watched her every move. She was sad, her head hung, only glancing up to me for a second to meet my gaze. She got in her car and pulled out. I took a deep breath and followed behind her, watching her in her mirror. I had to make her understand. I had to make her believe me no matter what the cost. No one was going to come between us. Not the school, not Jeff, and certainly not fucking Abby. Emma was mine. Now that I had her, nothing was going to keep us apart. Nothing.

Chapter Twenty-Four

As we pulled up to my place, my heart began to race. What if she changed her mind? What if she told me to fuck off and never come around her again? I hit the button on my visor, and the bay door opened. She slowly pulled her car inside. I glanced around at the empty road and pulled in after her, closing the door behind us.

I got out of my car and watched her slowly exit hers. I made my way over to the stairs, pausing for her to come closer. As she did, I walked up with her trailing behind me. Every step felt like I was getting closer to losing her. I opened the door and let her walk past me. She looked around as if she had never been there before. As if everything was different. I swallowed hard.

"I'll tell you everything you want to know." I searched her eyes, trying desperately to figure out what she was thinking.

"Do you still love her?" Her voice shook under the weight of her words.

"I don't know," I lied. I knew I hated her more than anything on this planet. What I didn't know was how I felt about Emma. I was drawn to her. I desperately wanted to consume every part of her like fire. What I didn't know is if that was love. It had been so long since I felt anything for anyone besides hatred.

I stepped closer to her. Her back straightened as I reached over to place my palm on her cheek. I could feel the heat rising off of her delicate skin. She leaned into my hand, closing her eyes. *Mine.* I knew exactly what I needed to say to keep her. It was written all over her sad little face.

"I do know that I love you more than anything." The words scared me as I spoke them, an emotion I didn't anticipate. Her eyes flew open, and she searched my face, trying to figure out if she had heard me correctly. "I love you. I wasn't sure it was even possible for me to care about anyone else again, but I can't deny how I feel about you." A wolf parading around in sheep's clothing, taunting the deer to play. I leaned close enough that I could feel her warmth. "Breathe," I whispered. She did as she was told. Her eyes continued to search mine and she didn't speak. "What else do you want to know?" I tried to hide the coldness in my voice.

"I think you said all I needed to hear." Her words melted me. I smiled and kissed her, desperate to feel her. There was a new passion in her that I wanted. I wanted everything she could give. I wrapped my fingers in her hair and tugged, holding her against my mouth as I let my other hand slip down the curve of her spine. Her body relaxed against mine. She pushed against my chest, her hands moving up to my neck. I let her touch me. She needed to know I was here and I wasn't going anywhere.

"Make love to me," she panted. I picked her up and carried her into my room. We couldn't go back upstairs yet. It was too soon. I needed to start over with her more slowly. We stripped off our clothes and tossed them aside.

"Are you sure this is what you want?" I didn't need to ask. I knew by the way she kissed me, the look in her eyes. I asked for her benefit. She needed to feel in control even though it was a lie.

"Yes, sir," she moaned. I kissed her, needing to taste her. Getting what I wanted, giving her what she needed.

"What do you want me to do to you?"

"Kiss me...here." Her fingers wrapped in my hair and tugged, guiding me to her breasts. She arched her back, pushing into my mouth. She was loving the control, the power. How could she not? There was no greater feeling. Not even love. I traced tiny circles over her, letting my teeth slide against her nipple. She moaned loudly. The sound vibrated in her chest, against my lips.

"Where else?" I panted, looking up to see her face twisted in pleasure. She held my hair and guided me lower. I licked my way down her stomach, dipping my tongue into her navel. I kept my eyes on her, watching her bite her lip and struggling to keep control.

"Please," she begged as I breathed against her sex. Begging me. *Mine.* Her having control was an illusion. I kissed her inner thigh. Her back arched again. I smiled against her skin. Slowly, I moved closer, pausing a moment before skimming my tongue across her center. She pushed back against me, nearly coming undone. I licked again and again as her hips moved with the rhythm of my mouth. I slid a finger into her hot wetness as I continued. She fisted the sheets, trying to keep from falling off the earth. I slid in another and increased my speed.

"Cum for me," I commanded. Her body immediately obeyed, tightening around me. She moaned as she circled her hips, fucking my fingers. As her body began to calm down, I climbed on top of her, pushing my cock against her entrance. "You belong to me, Emma." She stared at me, cheeks flushed. I rocked my hips so I would brush against her folds. She gasped as an aftershock of pleasure shot through her. "Tell me." I pushed, slowly slipping inside of her.

"I belong to you," she breathed. I pushed into her hard, claiming what was mine.

"Good girl," I breathed in her ear, letting my teeth skim her earlobe. Her hands trailed down my back, her nails scraping my skin. I moved faster, harder.

"I love you." Her voice uravelled me. My body shook and convulsed as hers tightened around my cock. I spilled myself inside of her, my Emma.

I relaxed against her, brushing the hair from her sweat-kissed skin. Nothing else mattered. I had her, and I wasn't going to let anyone take her from me.

Chapter Twenty-Five

I kept my position on top of her as I listened to her breathing grow quieter and slow. Eventually, it grew heavier, and I knew she had fallen asleep beneath me. I kissed her gently on the forehead and slipped off the bed. I grabbed my pants and pulled them on, glancing back at Emma who had not moved.

I walked out to the kitchen and poured myself a glass of bourbon before calling Stephen.

"We have a problem." I swirled my drink in the glass before gulping it down, enjoying the burn. Stephen sighed heavily in my ear.

"She's back." It wasn't a question. He was simply speaking his worst fear. I poured another drink, nodding to myself.

"*She* is back." I drank again as my eyes stayed fixed on the bedroom door, listening for any sounds from Emma.

"You can't let her destroy everything I have. Everything you have." I knew I had the mayor's attention.

"That's why I called." I tipped the bottle to my mouth.

"I'll be there in ten." I heard the line go dead. I tossed my phone on the counter and rested my head in my hands. Emma groaned in her sleep. I made my way back to my room and looked in. She was still sleeping peacefully as my world began to crumble around me. I sighed and pulled the bedroom door closed slowly.

Stephen was right on time. I let him in and gestured to the room so he knew to be quiet. I explained my relationship with Emma, and he looked at me disapprovingly but didn't say so.

"Why did she come back? Is it money? Is she going to say something?" He was panicked. I could sympathize. That night in our hotel a few years back hung fresh in my mind.

Abby loved the power she had over me—at least the power she thought she had over me. Truth was I was never one to listen to others. I had met Stephen in the tenth grade. I was well into cocaine to numb the pain or lack of feeling. I hung out at a park a few blocks from my house, selling some coke on the side. Misery loves company. Stephen was walking his dog one day who had gotten loose. I saw him dart across the park. I jumped from the old wooden picnic table and chased the dog down. We hung out almost every day after that. I shared my drugs, and he gave me someone to talk to—to really talk to.

When I began seeing Abby, he became jealous and distant that I was spending all of my free time with her. He called me late one night crying and mumbling incoherently. I was worried he had gotten some bad stuff, so I had Abby take me over to a hotel he and I often stayed at when we went on benders.

"Wait in the car." I looked at her for a moment to make sure she would comply. Abby looked terrified; part of that was probably due to the drugs. She nodded and I got out of the car and made my way across the dark parking lot. I spotted Stephen as he stepped outside. His clothes were askew, and he was on the verge of a full-on breakdown.

"What the fuck is going on, man?" I asked as he stared at me in terror. He opened the door, and I stepped in, scanning the lot before closing the door behind us. There it was. The beginning of our end. In the center of the twin-sized bed laid a girl. Her hair was knotted and tangled. Her skin was a pale grey.

"What the fuck did you do?" I could barely speak. My mouth was incredibly dry. I rushed to her side and put my fingers on her neck. At first I felt nothing. I stared at him, his eyes locked onto mine. "Shit."

"What? What? What is it?" He was losing control of himself.

"I think I felt something." There it was, a dull thump underneath the pads of my fingers.

"She has to go to the the hospital." His hand flew over his mouth then through his hair. I jumped off the bed and to him, backing him against the wall.

"What do you suppose she will say?" I locked eyes with him, hoping he was sober enough to listen. "Where do you think she will say she was? Who she was with?" I knew there was nothing stopping her from implicating Stephen. He was weak and it would take no time at all for him to sing my name like a canary. His hands fell to his sides as he thought about it. He stared off into nothing. I backed away from him slowly and turned back toward the bed. I brushed the girl's hair away from her face and picked up a pillow. She didn't fight, didn't move at all. I held it there over her mouth and waited. Unfortunately, that was the moment Abby decided to check on us. She stood in the door, terrified and high. Her body pressed tightly against the wood before she slid back out in the darkness. I nodded at Stephen and took off after her.

I closed the gap between us quickly. As she reached her car, I was able to grab her wrist and spin her around. Her back was against her door as she stared in shock into my eyes. For the first time she saw nothing staring back at her. I was on a much bigger high than cocaine could have ever taken me on. I was in control.

It wasn't easy, but I was able to convince her that I could help her in exchange for her silence.

I left clues around so that even the most neglectful of parents would be able to figure out I was carrying on an affair with my teacher. My father, predictable as ever, took the bait. He offered Abby two million dollars to never see me again. She took it without hesitation. I really had liked Abby.

She kept her word and never told anyone. She disappeared from my life, and Stephen and I went on to college. Eventually Abby's money ran out, and her coke addiction only grew. She found me and begged for more. She was a sad, pathetic mess. I wouldn't give her any more money. Instead, I offered to take care of her if she stayed with me.

It worked for a few months. Her habit had gone down to just getting high once or twice a week. We were finally able to get past everything that had happened. One night she had taken a pregnancy test, and it came back positive. We went straight to Vegas and got married, and she swore to never do any drugs again.

Three weeks later I found her in the bathroom wedged between the toilet and the bathtub. She was cold and sweaty, and her thighs were smeared with blood.

She couldn't resist the drugs. I hadn't seen her since then. Not until today.

I looked at Stephen in his tailored suit and perfectly combed hair. He had left the past where it belonged and become a highly respected mayor.

"She wants two million," I said as I poured us both a drink. Stephen drank his quickly, gasping as it burned his throat. I motioned for him to join me in the living room. We sat, staring at each other for a few minutes.

"I can help, but…fuck…two million?" His face twisted as he tried to come up with a plan. "How can we make her go away?"

The bedroom door squeaked, and we both turned around to see a shocked Emma wearing nothing but a T-shirt. She made her way toward the living room, oblivious to our presence. I stood and her eyes caught mine then went to Stephen's.

"This is Emma," I said, giving Stephen a hard look. Emma tugged at her shirt as she turned a beautiful shade of rose. "Emma, this is Mayor Locklin."

"Pleasure," Stephen said, trying not to stare.

"I'm gonna…" Her voice trailed off in embarrassment. She ducked back into my bedroom and closed the door. I turned to Stephen; my expression grew serious.

"She can't know," I whipsered. Stephen nodded. He knew the consequences if anyone found out. The door opened again.

"Emma," I called for her to join us.

"Shit," she muttered and bit her lip as she came to my side. I pulled her lip free from her teeth with my thumb.

"Sit." She took her seat on the couch.

"Emma." Stephen nodded his head to greet her.

"Mayor Locklin," she replied, ducking her head so he would not see her embarrassment.

"Please, call me Stephen," he stated, and she began to relax.

"Stephen," she repeated. I sat next to her and put my hand on her knee. *Mine.*

"Stephen is an old friend of mine from college. He also owes me a favor, which makes him trustworthy." I smiled at her, trying to make her more comfortable.

"Now, how do you propose we get rid of your ex-wife?" Stephen asked casually, not being careful with his words. I shot him a warning glare as I felt Emma grow limp at my side. "What the fuck?" Stephen screamed in a panic. I shook Emma, praying she would wake up.

"Emma!" I shook her. She groaned but didn't open her eyes. "Get some water!" I shouted at Stephen. He ran to the kitchen and filled a glass, bringing it back to me. I splashed water on her face, and her eyes began to flutter.

"What happened?" she asked, looking around, confused.

"Are you narcoleptic?" Stephen asked, looking genuinely scared shitless.

"No," she answered, tugging at her shirt. I placed my hand on her shoulder to soothe her.

"We didn't mean 'get rid of her' like that." I had to hold back a laugh. It was *exactly* what we meant. "We just need to figure out how to make her not come back again and again once she has been paid." I rubbed her knee, trying to make sure she believed me. She looked to Stephen.

"Right, well, we need to negotiate terms and have your lawyer speak with her. Are you sure this is about the money and not about some sort of revenge?" he asked, his eyes burning through me.

"No, no. She's the one who broke my heart, remember?" I glared at him. He was saying too much.

"Yeah, I know. I just needed to make sure there was nothing else that would come out later." He stood up and I rose from the couch. "Should be a pretty straightforward arrangement. Are you sure you want to pay her off? You could always let her say what she wants. It's not like you need the teaching job." I ran my hands through my hair and nodded. I knew he was really asking if I thought she would go through with it—if she would spill everything.

"You know I can't let this come out. I would never hear the end of it from my father."

"I'll help as much as I can. I owe you that much," Stephen replied, holding out his hand. We shook and then he nodded at Emma politely before leaving. I followed after him and locked the door.

"You could have warned me that you had company!" She smacked me playfully on the arm.

"You could have warned me that you pass out so easily. Had that happened in the bedroom I would have thought I killed you." My mind flashed to the hotel.

"Sorry." She looked down at her feet. I stepped closer, pulling her into my arms and squeezing her tightly.

"Can I ask you something?"

I took a deep breath, my arms stiffened. "Ask away."

"What did you do for the mayor that he feels he owes you?" She looked up to me.

"If it wasn't for me, he would have never made it through college. I tutored him, helped keep him on track." I smiled at her and squeezed her closer.

"Here I thought you helped him bury a hooker or something." She joked. I laughed and stared over her.

"No, the dead hookers didn't start to pile up until after he became mayor." She bit her lip and slapped me playfully on the chest.

"Where are you going to come up with the kind of money she is asking for on a professor's salary?" she asked. I let go of her and ran my hands though my hair. She was asking too many questions.

"My father. In fact, he is the reason she and I didn't last in the first place." I shook my head. "Abby started tutoring me senior year. I was more into hanging out with my friends and getting in trouble. I didn't take my grades seriously. One night one thing lead to another. I'll spare you the details, but my father found out that we were seeing each other. He went to Abby and offered her money to stay away from me." I stared off at the wall. "She took it and never looked back. To add insult to injury, she began flaunting some new guy around town. Everywhere I went I saw them together. It wasn't until college when she called me and begged for me to come see her. We dated for a few months." I glanced down at the floor. "We ran off to Vegas on a whim and got married. Everything was perfect again until I found out my father had paid her. She begged for me to stay with her, but I couldn't. Now she wants to make my life miserable." I looked her in the eyes to gauge her reaction.

"I'm so sorry." She stepped closer, but I put up my hand to stop her.

"I don't want to be pitied, Emma. It was a long time ago. I just want this bitch out of my life once and for all."

"So, if your father is rich, why are you working as a professor?"

"I don't know. I tutored all through college, and I really enjoyed it." I smiled. "Plus, I like to be in control, but I'm sure you noticed that. I don't want to ever get hurt like that again."

I ran my fingers down the length of her jaw and smacked her playfully on her bottom with my other hand.

"Ouch!" She jumped, and I pulled her body against mine.

"I think I answered enough questions for one day." I ran my thumb over her bottom lip.

We spent the next few hours in bed together.

"Go take a nice long bath. I'll make us something to eat." I kissed her on the forehead and made my way into the kitchen to prepare something to eat.

"That smells delicious!" she said as she sat down at the kitchen island and twirled her wet hair into a bun.

"Thanks." I sat a plate down in front of her. Cheese ravioli in a mushroom sauce—one of my favorite dishes. I watched her clean her plate, and I could barely stand to eat a bite.

"Not hungry?" she asked, pulling me from my thoughts.

"I was just thinking about how money changes people." *Lie.* Money doesn't change people. You are either good or bad, kind or greedy, dominant or submissive. Her eyebrows knitted together as she thought that over.

"I wouldn't do that to you. I'm not that kind of person. I'm not her," she said, putting her hand on mine. She thought I was talking about Abby. I laced my fingers in hers and gave her hand a squeeze. After a moment, she let go of my hand and went off to the bedroom. She reappeared with her cell phone pressed to her ear.

Chapter Twenty-Six

"Aunt Judy? I won't be home tonight." She smiled at me. She ended the call and set the phone down, raising her eyebrow at me. She turned and walked toward the elevator. She stepped inside and disappeared behind the doors.

I got up from my stool and rinsed our dishes in the sink. I grabbed the bourbon and poured a quick drink as I thought of Emma alone upstairs. I smirked and emptied my glass, setting it back down on the counter. I headed toward the elevator. My pulse began to race as I got closer. The doors opened and I gave myself a minute for my eyes to adjust. Then I saw her, spread out on a table and waiting for me. *Perfection.* I began to unhook my belt as I drank in her beauty.

"You certainly know how to make me feel better," I said as I slid my pants over my hips. I began at her feet, nibbling at her arches and running my fingers up her instep. She pulled against the restraints. I kissed my way up her calves, making sure to touch every part of her body.

"Do you want me?" I asked as my lips skimmed over her inner thigh to the sensitive aread just below her center.

"Yes," her body bucked off the table. I licked my lips and continued to place a trail of kisses over her hip bones and across her lower stomach.

"Yes, what?" I asked as I dipped my tongue into her navel, making my way to her chest.

"Yes, sir," she panted.

I moved closer to her left breast. I slipped my hand between us. She pushed back against my fingers. She was already slick with wanting. I held my hand still and let her rub against me. I took her nipple between my teeth and gently bit down. She gasped and I released it, swirling my tongue against her.

"Please," she begged as her hips began to move faster.

"Tell me you love me." Her breathing quickened, and I knew she was on the verge of cumming. "Say it," I whispered in her ear as I hovered over her. She pulled against the restraints. "Say it!" I ordered.

"I love you," she panted. I thrust myself into her, and she cried out at the sudden pain. I didn't slow. I needed this and she was willing to give it to me.

"I love you," I whispered in her ear. Her body pulsed and tightened around me. I thrust into her again. Again. I finished, falling lazily on top of her. I trailed kisses over her face as I undid her wrists. Once freed, her arms wrapped around my neck and held my mouth to hers.

My phone rang out in the darkness. Her arms squeezed me tighter.

"I have to get it. It may be my lawyer." Her arms relaxed and I was able to get up. I answered my phone as I watched her unlock her ankles. My lawyer rambled in my ear about payoffs. I watched her slip on her clothes. It was justas big of a turn on as when she took them off. I put my hand on the small of her back and led her to the elevator.

"I don't give a fuck about the money. I want her out of my life." I ran my hands through my hair. If the money didn't keep her away, I would find a more permanent solution. We stepped out of the elevator, and Emma headed for the bathroom. I sighed, relieved to have some privacy.

"There is nothing to stop her from coming back for more. I can't help you if you don't tell me what is going on," Mr. Daniels pleaded with me. I gritted my teeth.

"What the fuck do I pay you for?" I growled and threw the phone on the couch. I sunk down, resting my head in my hands.

I didn't hear Emma coming. I felt the couch sink down next to me, and her hand rubbed my back. I sat up and grabbed her wrist.

"Don't," I hissed. She looked at me as if I had stabbed her in the heart. She pulled back and slid across the couch.

"It's OK," she whispered. "You have a lot on your mind." I shook my head. I was pushing away the one person I wanted to protect.

"I know it's not fair to you, and I am trying, but it is hard for me to get close to people," I explained. It also wasn't *safe* for me to get close to people. Not for them anyway.

"I'm here, no matter how long it takes. I'm not going any-where." I wanted to believe every word of what she said, but I had heard it all before and was too scared to give my complete trust. I looked her in the eye and nodded. "So…what did your lawyer have to say?" Her face was sad with worry.

"He doesn't think I should pay her. He thinks I should give up my job." I looked away, wondering if I could change things, would I?

"What do you want to do?" She leaned closer but still kept a reasonable distance between us.

"I don't know. I don't want to give her another fucking dime, but I don't want to quit my job. She wins either way." I threw my hands in the air. I should have let her rot on that bathroom floor. She would have died soon enough had I not thought the baby could be saved.

I knew what I had to do, but I wasn't sure I could face her and not lay hands on her. I grabbed my phone and paced the floor as I called.

"I'll get you the fucking money, but if I ever see your face again, or if you come near Emma, I will fucking kill you." I meant every fucking word of it.

"Will, I...you...you don't mean that." She was on the verge of tears. If I was going to make her cry, I wanted it to be in person so I could watch. I hung up the phone and headed into my room to grab my shoes and a jacket. I was going to put an end to this now.

"Where are we going?" *To hell* was the first thing that crossed my mind. Emma was off the couch and walking toward me.

"You are staying here." It wasn't up for debate. I cupped her face in my hands and tried to soften my expression." I am going to go pay Abby and get her out of our lives." I kissed her softly on the forehead, holding it an extra second just in case it was the last time. I wanted to kill Abby. I wanted to ensure she would never be a problem again. "Have you thought anymore about where we are going after graduation?" I asked, trying to direct her thoughts elsewhere.

She looked confused. "What?"

"You still want to go?" She must have assumed I only asked her because of the note. She had no idea the other skeletons in my closet.

"Of course. Why wouldn't I? Just pick someplace warm. I want you naked as much as possible." I grinned wickedly and turned to leave. "Don't answer the door for anyone." I warned and locked it. I knew I couldn't kill Abby, at least not now. I had left a trail, starting with my lawyer that leads to my front door. I would have to use a different approach.

I called Stephen and told him to come get me. I pulled Emma's car around the corner while I waited, just in case someone stopped by. He arrived moments later, and we made our way downtown. Crowds were forming waiting to get into clubs. Where there were partiers, there would be drugs. I parked and walked up to two young guys hanging on the corner by the liquor shop.

"Hey, you holding?" I asked with a nod. One of the guys walked behind me, looking for anyone who might be within earshot. He came back and nodded to his buddy.

"Yeah, man. Whatchu need?"

I wiped my nose to make it look more believable. I had done this many times in the past and knew how to play the game.

"Hook me up with an 8 ball." We made the exchange, and I shoved it in my pocket quickly and headed back to Stephen's car.

"What the fuck? What are you doing?" He was terrified. I didn't expect anything different from Stephen. I was the one always looking out for the both of us.

"I'm going to kill her with kindness," I said, giving him a hard look. We pulled off and didn't speak another word. I texted Abby and got the location for the meet. I knew it would be a hotel, since she still lived in California. How fitting. Her message came back that she was at Seaside Motel. It was only a few blocks away. I had been there a time or two before.

We pulled into the parking lot as my phone rang. It was Emma.

"What's wrong?" I asked, glancing over at Stephen who pretended to be distracted by something outside of the car.

"Angela is here!" she whispered in a panic.

"Shit. She probably saw my car downstairs and thinks I am avoiding her."

"Your car is downstairs? How did you…"

"Stephen picked me up. He wanted to go with me for the exchange of money. Just stay inside and be quiet. She will leave soon." I hoped she wouldn't question me further. Stephen and I were in this mess together and would finish it that way.

"OK. What about my car?" I could hear knocking at the door in the background.

"I moved it before I left. It is parked around the building. Emma, I'm sorry about all of this." I waited for a reply, clenching my jaw.

"No worries," she said, and after a moment the line went dead. Stephen looked at me for confirmation that we were going through with this. I nodded and got out of the car.

I walked inside one of the side doors and made my way to room 213. Abby answered, leaning flirtatiously on the door, wearing a short skirt and tight white tank, no bra. I looked her up and down, and she smiled before holding the door open wide for me to go in.

"I missed you," she purred. I could tell she had been drinking. I didn't turn around or respond. She came up behind me and slid her hand around me, running it down my stomach. "You bring me something?" I knew she was anxious to get her hands on the cash. I didn't bring any.

"Of course I did." I turned around slowly and pulled the coke from my pocket. "For old time's sake." I grinned. She put her hands up to refuse, but she bit her lip, and I knew it wouldn't take much to persuade her.

"Come on, Abby." I stepped closer. "If I recall, you and I had some pretty good times."

She smiled and brushed her hair back from her face.

"Just a taste?" I asked, raising an eyebrow. She giggled and nodded her head. "Good girl." I made my way over to the dresser and began cutting lines. Abby put on some low music and poured us a drink. I drank my shot and pulled a one hundred dollar bill from my wallet. I rolled it between my fingers and held it out to her. "Ladies first." She giggled and licked her lips, staring into my eyes. I smiled back and nudged the bill closer to her. She took it like an excited kid at Christmas. I knew once I got her started she wouldn't be able to stop. She glanced back at me one last time before the line disappeared beneath her. She sat up, touching her fingertips to her nose as her eyes fluttered.

"Thank you," she said as she passed me the bill.

"There is nothing I wouldn't do…" I grinned. *She had no idea.* I took the bill from her hand. I had committed at least nine crimes already today; one more wouldn't change anything. My thoughts flashed to Emma. I saw her smiling, biting her lip. I closed my eyes and leaned over, snorting my line quickly.

"Yeah!" Abby wrapped her arms around my neck from behind. "I've missed this. I've missed us." I didn't say anything. I held the bill over my shoulder for her. She took it without hesitation. Her next line was gone in an instant as I fixed myself another drink. "Your turn."

I held up my drink to signal I was already in the midst of my own party. She pouted, sticking out her bottom lip like a child.

"One vice at a time," I joked and drank from my glass.

"Suit yourself." She shrugged and did the next one for me. As she stood up she stumbled backward, barely catching herself before she fell. I had her where I needed her.

"I have to get going," I said, checking my watch.

"Ohh, you can't leave me here all alone." She sounded desperate. Pathetic. She crossed the room, shaking her hips and trying her best to look sexy. "The fun was just beginning." Her arms snaked around my waist.

"I'll make it up to you. I'll order room service. Anything you like." *A witness to see you alive and alone.* She smiled wide, unable to refuse anything for free. I guided her to the phone and dialed for her but let her place the order. I knew nothing would likely happen to her tonight, but it was important to cover all of the bases. I waited until she hung up before leaving some money on the dresser next to the remainder of the cocaine.

"Aren't you forgetting something?" she called from behind me. I turned around to see her fingers sliding over her chest.

"It will take a few days to get the money together. You didn't expect me to carry two million in my pocket, did you?" She bit her lip, struggling to focus.

"So, I'll see you again?" she asked, running her hand through her hair.

"Whatever it takes." I smiled and left quickly, knowing she wouldn't be able to resist the drugs. I also left enough extra money for her to purchase more if she survived tonight.

I made my way to Stephen's car.

"Well?" he asked, sounding more panicked than before.

"I took care of it," I said as he pulled out into traffic. He looked like he had seen a ghost.

"You didn't…" his voice trailed off, unable to say the words.

"She's alive…for now," I said. He didn't ask anything else, just took me home.

Chapter Twenty-Seven

❦

J found Emma curled up in a ball on the couch. I slipped my arms under her and lifted her from the couch to carry her to bed. She stretched and yawned. "Shhh," I whispered.

"What time is it?" she asked, looking around.

"Just after three in the morning." I laid her down on the center of my bed.

"How did everything go?" She pulled the covers over her as she watched me take off my clothes. I thought over how to respond.

"She has the money. Everything is taken care of." It was. With the money I gave her, Abby could fuel her addiction. I slipped into bed behind Emma, pressing my body against hers. She relaxed against me and drifted back off to sleep moments later. I was not as fortunate. I stayed awake for another hour or so, tracing the line of her hip bone as I worried about what would happen next. When I did sleep, I had horrible nightmares of life without Emma—her finding out my secrets and never wanting to be near me again.

Early in the morning I awoke to the sounds of my phone vibrating against the wood of the dresser. I slipped myself out from under the covers and pulled on my jeans. I grabbed the phone and headed for the kitchen to make some coffee.

"Yeah?" I asked, rubbing the sleep from my eyes.

"I'm worried this plan of yours is going to backfire." Stephen was panicked and his voice sounded as if he slept worse than I had, without the coke to make his thoughts race.

"It will work," I said quietly as Emma rounded the corner. I put my finger to her lips to keep her quiet. She smirked and went to the cupboard to get herself a cup for her morning coffee.

"What if it doesn't?" He was pleading with me like a child to tell him everything was going to be OK. That the monster in his closet wasn't real; but I was that monster.

"You have my word it will be taken care of," I assured him. Emma reached for the sugar that sat on the counter in front of me. I pushed it back out of her reach and gave her a devilish smile. She made a face at me. She reached again and again I pushed it farther. She lifted her body up so her feet came off the floor and reached again. I closed the gap between us, pressing myself against her backside.

"I'll call you back," I said to Stephen and hung up. I set the phone down and slid my fingers down her sides, gripping her hips and pulling her back into me. Her fingers gripped the edge of the counter. I slowly looped my fingers in her panties and pulled them down. I leaned over her and whispered in her ear. "Don't let go." I pushed against her entrance, slowly letting myself slide in. I rocked slowly against her. Gripping her hipbones. She moaned quietly. "You like it when I fuck you nice and slow?" I asked, saying the words in time with my thrusts.

"Yes, sir," she moaned and her back arched, allowing me to go deeper. I did. "Aaahh," she breathed. I slid my hand up the length of her spine and tangled my fingers in her hair, pulling back gently. I began to move faster, filling her completely. "You feel so good inside of me." Her words burned. My good girl begging to be fucked. Her walls tightened around me, sending us both tumbling over the edge of ecstasy. I continued to rock my hips until the last shutter of pleasure rippled through her body. I released her hair and she lay her head down on the countertop, exhausted. I stepped back and admired the beautiful view. I brought my hand down across her backside. She screamed and arched her back. I quickly dipped my fingers between her thighs and rubbed lightly over her wetness. I wasn't finished with her yet. I lay back over her and gently nipped her earlobe. "Mmmm." The sound of wanting escaped her lips.

"This," I let a finger slip inside of her and pulled back out, "belongs to me" I rubbed her slowly in small circles, again and again.

"Yes." Her fingers held tightly to the edge of the countertop.

"Say it." I let my finger slide back inside of her. She pushed back against me, eager for more.

"*It* belongs to you," she moaned. I laughed at her sudden shyness.

"Your pussy belongs to me." I slipped a second finger inside of her. "Say it," I breathed into her ear.

"My pussy belongs to you." She was willing to do anything. I smiled as I slipped my other hand around her waist. I rubbed against her front with one hand while fucking her with the fingers from the other. She tightened around me, pulling them deeper as she panted, unraveling again.

I gripped her hips and pulled back off the counter. She leaned against it, steadying herself. I slid her cup of coffee over to her.

"Sugar is on the counter." I smirked and went to my room to get dressed for the day.

The morning went by without a hitch. Angela had not shown up to work today and very few people were talking about Jeff's accident. When it came time for Emma's class, I felt like the world was no longer fighting against us. I watched her walk in my room like an angel who had just walked through the gates of heaven. My heaven. I mingled with the students, answering questions about graduation for a few minutes, but my thoughts never left her. I stared at her whenever possible, even taking a moment to smell her sweet scent on my fingers. A knock came at the door, and I immediately looked to Emma. She was stricken with panic. I ran my hands through my hair, wondering what it would be to end my beautiful fantasy. The accident from my past? Jeff's crash? Angela? Abby?

I walked to the door and stepped outside, coming face-to-face with Angela. She was the lesser of all of my evils.

"What?" I asked as I ran my hands through my hair again.

"Can I stay with you? For a few days?" she asked, tucking her hair nervously behind her ear.

"Stay with your husband." I was in no mood for this.

"William…" Her voice trailed off, and she said nothing more.

"Don't ever come to my place again. You're not welcome there," I warned her and went back inside my room. I continued my lecture where I had left off, not letting my gaze fall on Emma for too long.

She didn't stay after class. I had wanted her to, but it would be foolish to risk what we had when I was so close to being able to be with her forever. I made it through the last few mindnumbing classes without a hitch.

When the day finally came to a close, I couldn't wait to be close to her, to touch her. I made it to my car and scanned the parking lot. She was just slipping into her seat. I pulled out my phone and sent her a quick message.

Where are you headed?

I got inside my car and waited.

Home.

Mine?

My aunt is going to start asking questions if I don't show up every once and awhile.

As my eyes danced over her words, Angela made her way to the side of my car. I clenched my jaw, debating on whether or not to take her up on wanting to stay with me just so I could get rid of her.

"This is starting to border on stalking," I said, half-joking.

"Wlliam, I'm not trying to cause you any trouble. I need help. I can't stay with my husband anymore." Her eyes swelled with tears. I watched Emma drive by, not looking at me. My heart sank. I have had about enough of Angela upsetting her.

"That's not my problem." I clenched my jaw, biting back the things I really wanted to say. One tear escaped her eye, and her jaw quivered.

"Please, if you ever cared about me at all…" I glared at her, and her mouth snapped shut. She took a silent step back from my car, and I pushed it in drive. I left her standing alone in the lot. I texted Emma to make sure she didn't have the wrong idea.

Angela means nothing to me, you know that right?

Emma, please answer me. Fucking answer me.

She didn't respond. I would have gladly listened to her yell and scream than to completely ignore me. Everything seemed to collide together at once. I had to see her, had to make this right. I drove to her house, parking up the road out of sight.

I made my way to the back of her house so I could sneak in her bedroom window, but there she lay, tanning herself in the sun.

"You are going to burn that pretty little ass of yours," I said, taking in the view of her laying on her stomach, small scraps of fabric covering her most private parts. *Mine.* She jumped at the sound of my voice and flipped over to her back.

"What are you doing here?" She didn't try to hide the irritation in her voice.

"You didn't respond. I got worried." She rolled her eyes at me. Rolled her fucking eyes at me.

"You didn't respond to me, either, and you don't see me acting like a stalker," she hissed angrily. I felt like her words were a slap in the face. *A fucking stalker? Was that what I was to her?*

"You're mad at me?" I asked, sinking down to my knees. I needed to make this right. "She doesn't mean anything to me. She's trying to work through her own feelings. She doesn't want to stay with her husband."

"I don't care about her marital woes. She brought that on herself," she shot back. I swallowed hard. She was jealous.

"Fair enough."

"I'm not mad at you, but you have to understand all of this is very new to me. I'm not exactly sure what we are doing here, but I know seeing you with Angela scared me," she explained. She didn't want to lose me. I leaned closer, running my hand over her side and onto the small of her back. I needed to touch her, to feel that she was real, that she was still mine.

"You have *nothing* to worry about." I searched her eyes for understanding." I won't ever hurt you, Emma. I promise. I will never talk to her again if that's what you want." I was on my knees begging her to stay with me.

"No, I trust you. I'm sorry, I just got a little jealous seeing you two together." She sighed. I pushed my lips against hers, letting my hand wrap in her hair. I wrapped around her tightly and squeezed, never wanting to let her go.

"I thought you were going to leave me," I confessed. At that moment I realized what she meant to me. I could never, would never, be without her.

"I'm not going anywhere, William." She pulled back to look in my eyes. "I love you." I kissed her again, wanting to drink in her words.

"I love you so much, Emma." I heard a noise from inside the house. We both glanced over.

"Go! I'll call you later," she said, kissing me quickly. I left, not wanting to risk being caught.

I made my way to my car and sat for a few minutes, running my hands through my hair. This girl was driving me fucking crazy. I couldn't get enough of her. I wanted her more than I wanted the air I breathe. My phone lit up and vibrated on the seat next to me.

My aunt left for the night.

I smiled and got out of the car, looking around to make sure no one saw me. I walked to her front door and slipped inside. I could hear the water running from the shower down the hall. I made my way to the door. I gripped the shower curtain and slowly pulled it back, revealing Emma's backside dripping with water. I immediately grew hard.

"You are so beautiful," I said as I rubbed my hand over the front of my jeans. She smiled over her shoulder.

"You think you could wash my back for me?" she asked, biting her lip. I smiled and began peeling off my clothes. I stepped in behind her, pressing the length of myself against her. I reached around and grabbed her bath sponge from her and slowly slid it down her neck. Her head fell to the side, and I pulled the sponge down over her shoulder, circling it down her chest and over her breasts. She sucked in a ragged breath, causing me to twitch against her ass. I slid it lower, down over her belly and in between her legs. She moaned, putting her hands on the wall in front of her for balance.

"Spread your legs," I ordered. I slid the sponge against her, making sure my fingers brushed against her. She panted, pushing back against my hand. I ran the sponge down the length of her legs and made sure to soap every part of her body. She returned the favor by soaping up my body as well. Her hands glided over my chest and over the muscles of my stomach. Her hand moved lower. I watched her as her eyes gazed back at me, washing me clean.

We rinsed off and got out. I waited for Emma to hand me a towel as I stared at my own reflection in the mirror. I didn't recognize the person I was becoming, but I didn't hate it either. We began to dry ourselves, and my gaze shifted to her.

"What?" she asked, her cheeks a lovely shade of pink.

"You're beautiful," I said, wrapping my towel around my hips. I reached out and took hers from her. I began to slowly wipe the water droplets that clung to her skin. She smiled and closed her eyes, trusting me completely. I finished by running it over her hair. "Perfect," I sighed. I kissed her on the cheek and wrapped the towel around her, tucking it into itself. "Have you thought about where you want to go after graduation?" I wanted to drag her away from this place.

"Well." She walked past me toward her room. "I was thinking about the Carolinas." She dropped her towel and grabbed a pair of panties out of her drawer.

"I was thinking outside of the States." I watched her slide the underwear up her legs.

"I don't know if that's a good idea." She gave me a sideways glance. That was the response I anticipated.

"OK. How about the West Coast?" I asked, sliding my hand across her stomach from behind, trailing kisses across her shoulder.

"That sounds nice." She laid her head over, and I kissed up her neck. She wrapped her fingers in my hair, tugging gently. I let my hand run lower, dipping a finger under the waistband of her panties.

"William?" She turned to look at me. "Do you trust me?" It was a loaded question. I did. Not with all of my secrets, but with my heart.

"Yes," I whispered, searching her eyes. She turned to face me, placing her hands on my chest and pushing me slowly back toward her bed. Feeling the mattress touch my legs, I sat down, looking up into her beautiful green eyes. She looped her fingers in her panties and slowly slid them down her thighs. She was inches from me when she bent over, and I couldn't resist the urge to taste her. I leaned forward, sucking one of her nipples into my mouth and running my teeth along it. She moaned, letting her body fall onto mine, her legs on either side of me. She placed a hand on my face, staring at me as her hips began to rock against my hardness.

"Oh, God." I grabbed her ass hard and moved her harder. Her wetness glided her against me effortlessly. Her eyes closed, and she was panting heavily. "Look at me." She obeyed. "I love you."

"I love you," she moaned as her body began to buck against me. "Ohh" I slowed her and held her tightly against me, stopping her from cumming.

"Not yet." I pushed her damp hair away so I could see her beautifully flushed face.

"Oh, God…please," she begged. I loved it when she begged. Her hand dipped down between us as she began to touch herself. I let my hips begin to rock again.

"I want to taste you." I glanced down at her hand and back to her eyes. She lifted her hand and ran her wet fingers along my lip. She dipped the tip of one of her fingers into my mouth, and I let a slow growl rumble from my chest. I lifted her and laid her back on the bed in one swift motion. I quickly found her nipple and sucked as she arched her back, pushing it further into my mouth. I kissed my way down her stomach, positioning myself between her legs. I let my tongue dip into her wetness, and she pushed herself against my mouth.

"William," she moaned my name, and it never sounded so sweet. I moaned back inside of her, slipping a finger into her as she pulsed and bucked against my lips. I crawled up the length of her body and entered her as she continued to cum, setting off my own orgasm. I relaxed against her, struggling to catch my breath as I ran my finger across her brow.

"What?" she asked.

"I just can't believe how lucky I am."

She grabbed my face and pulled my lips to hers.

Chapter Twenty-Eight

❧

J held her for hours while I watched her sleep. I still couldn't believe I was lucky enough to share a bed with her.

By three in the morning, I kissed her good-bye and left her a note so she would know I was thinking of her.

I miss you.
Love, William

I couldn't sleep when I got home, so I booked a flight for Emma and me for California. I was able to schedule it for the night of graduation.

The next few days flew by with relatively no problems. I managed to avoid anyone who had tried to come between Emma and me. I snuck private moments with Emma whenever I could. I even had a key made for her so she could come see me whenever she needed or wanted to. She exercised that right often.

I was anxious for the day to end so I could wrap my arms around Emma. As I opened the door to my place, a small piece of paper fluttered to the ground.

Before I kill you, I want you to watch her die.

I walked inside, anger bubbling within me. I placed the note on the counter, pouring myself a drink and staring at it. I didn't know what to do. I didn't know if I could protect her. I made my way to the couch and sat down, resting my head in my hands. This is what I deserved, I knew it, but Emma didn't ask for any of this. I heard her key slide into the lock of the door. I wanted to rush to her and push her away, but I didn't have the strength. I knew what I needed to do. I knew it would only put both of us in more danger.

"What's wrong?" she asked as she rushed to my side, careful to keep distance between us. I took a deep breath and held out the note for her. She deserved to know the danger I brought to her feet. She read it carefully, then let the paper fall from her fingers. "Oh my God," she whispered, her hands covering her mouth. I nodded but couldn't bring myself to look at her. "We have to call the police." Her voice was high-pitched, and I knew she was on the verge of going into shock. I narrowed my eyes. It was too late to go to the police. I had done too much.

"I'll take care of this," I said and got up, determined to put an end to this once and for all. Emma jumped to her feet and placed herself in my path, laying her hand on my chest. I glanced down at her delicate fingers then back to her. She recoiled, taking a step back.

"You can't go over there. You are going to do something you'll regret!" She was panicked, and concerned for me more so than Abby. I softened my expression, not wanting her to worry, not wanting her to know what I was capable of.

"I'm not going to do anything to her. I just want to end this thing once and for all." I locked eyes with her, pleading with her to trust me. I needed to take care of this, or we would never be able to be together. She bit her lip and stepped to the side. "Lock the door. Do not let anyone in this fucking house. I don't care if they are on fire. Do you understand?" She nodded and followed me to the door to lock it behind me.

I drove to the hotel I had met Abby at just days ago. I knocked several times before she answered. Her face was pale and drawn in; her eyes looked dead and lifeless. I pushed the door open further, and she stumbled back so I could enter.

"You really think you can threaten me and get away with it?" I asked, seething with anger. She looked at me shocked and dazed. She tripped over her own feet toward me. The smell of liquor wafted through the air. I glanced around and noticed she had given in to the temptation to buy more drugs. Powder dusted nearly every surface in the room. "It wasn't you?" I asked, not expecting a response. She rubbed her arms as if she was cold, but the room was muggy.

"You wanna..." Her voice trailed off. I shoved past her and made my way out of the room.

I pulled out my phone and shot a text to Emma.

It's not Abby. I am on my way.

She responded immediately.

Angela is here!!!!

Of course, it made sense.

Do NOT let her in!

I raced to my car and drove as fast as I could to get to Emma's side. It was a sick joke being played on me. I made it home in record time, flying to the steps as my phone rang.

"H-he's in the building…I think h-he killed her…don't come in here!" Emma's voice shook as she spoke. I made my way to the door.

"Emma, calm down. Breathe. No one is here."

"William!" Emma screamed from behind the door. There was no time to react. Something hard came down across my face, causing me to stumble. I recovered quickly and swung, connecting with the man's face. He stumbled backward but caught himself before falling down the steps. I noticed something on the steps leading to the third floor. It was a body. Just then the man swung again, hitting me hard in the stomach. I doubled over, struggling to breathe. I swung my arm, my elbow hitting him hard in the ribs. I grabbed him by his hair and brought his face-down on my knee, breaking his nose. Blood poured from his face as his arms swung wildly toward me. I wanted to kill him. I kicked out, my foot landing squarely on his chest, sending him flying to the landing below.

He didn't move again, so I ducked to the side and checked on Angela, certain she was dead. I brushed her hair back from her face, and she let out a small groan.

"She's alive!" I shouted to Emma.

"I'm sorry," Angela whispered, and her eyes were full of regret and pain. "He found out about us." I glanced behind me at the man who lay motionless on the landing below. I looked back at her and nodded. Her husband was not ready to give up his wife to someone else. I dialed the police and told them a watered down version of what had happened. Then I sent a text to Emma.

Go to the third floor and wait for me. Don't make a sound.

I waited a few minutes before helping Angela inside. She was battered and bruised, but I knew that she was going to be OK. I locked the door behind us just in case her husband regained consciousness. I wanted to finish him off, but that would have to wait for a different time. The cops arrived within a few minutes, and we both told them our versions of what had happened. As far as they were concerned her husband was a very jealous man who thought she was sleeping with everyone else. It didn't take long for them to haul him off and take Angela in to be checked out. I poured myself a drink and sent a text to Emma.

Come down, unless you want me to come up.

I smiled at the idea that she had just spent the better part of an hour on that floor alone. I heard the elevator door open, and I turned to see her. She ran across the room as fast as her feet could carry her. I wrapped my arms around her and lifted her off the ground.

"Shh." I ran my hand over her head. "It's over." She pulled back from me. "It's over," I said, staring into her eyes. She relaxed, leaning her forehead against mine.

"I was so worried."

"It was Angela's husband. The cops took him away. They took it as nothing more than a husband who suspected his wife of cheating. We're safe now." I kissed her forehead wanting to take away her fear.

"She knows." Her voice was soft, and I could tell she felt like she had let me down.

"She doesn't know who was in here. As far as she knows, it was a one-night stand and you left before she woke up." I shook my head.

"How is she?"

"They took her to the hospital to do some scans, but she is going to be fine." I rubbed her back for a moment before taking her in my arms and carrying her off to bed.

Chapter Twenty-Nine

$\mathcal{I}$ couldn't have been more proud of Emma as she crossed the stage to receive her diploma. She looked amazing. Her skin was glowing with happiness. The ceremony drug on, and I was dying to be able to touch her. After the diplomas where handed out and everyone cheered, students found their family and friends. I mingled with the crowd, making my way closer to her. She was engaging in a conversation about after-graduation trips when I walked behind her, making sure to graze her backside with my hand. I felt her body stiffen against my touch, and she smiled as I walked away, getting lost in the crowd.

"Good evening, sir," a voice called from behind me as someone touched my arm. I spun around and couldn't stop my jaw from falling open.

"J…What are you…" I couldn't even form a sentence. My eyes darted around, finding Emma still chatting with her friends.

"I know people outside of the club." She smiled and I swallowed hard, forcing myself to smile back at her. I ran my hand through my hair and lowered my voice. "No one can know," I said, my tone serious. She nodded quickly and leaned closer to me.

"Your secret is safe with me." She winked.

"It was a pleasure seeing you," I said politely and backed away into the crowd. She nodded and turned to walk away.

Emma hugged her friends and began walking in my direction. She smiled quickly then stopped face-to-face with Judy. I held my breath as I watched the exchange between them. Emma hadn't seen me speaking with her, had she? They only talked for a few minutes before J pulled her in for a hug. My stomach knotted as it finally sunk in. She was Emma's Aunt Judy, the one who had made her cry countless times and treated her like she was nothing. I felt my body temperature rise as anger coursed through my body.

I made my way to my car and sat in there a few minutes contemplating leaving and not coming back. Things had just gone from complicated to fucked up beyond words. Judy was on my list of people I wanted to remove from Emma's life for hurting her, but she knew one of my secrets. Something that Emma would never forgive me for. I put the car in drive and headed down the road to the pizza shop where I had planned to meet Emma.

She was already there waiting. I got out and slipped into the passenger side of her car. I kissed her hard, needing to feel her against me, not knowing how long I would be able to hold onto her.

"God, I love you." I pressed my forehead against hers, inhaling her intoxicating scent. "Are you ready?" I asked, holding my breath. She nodded and I wasted no time getting out and retrieving her bags for her. She followed, slipping into the passenger seat of my car. I laced my fingers in hers, and we drove off toward the airport.

We arrived early in the afternoon at LAX. I held Emma's hand as we made our way to the baggage claim. I hadn't been able to break the physical connection between us for the entire trip. I wrapped my arms around her, pulling her body flush against me. *Mine.* I was addicted to her. To her touch, her smell. No one bothered us. No one cared that we were together. We were just another couple on vacation. I pulled her through the crowd, anxious to get her alone. The sun was bright, and we waited outside for our car. I spotted my driver a moment later holding up a sign with my name on it. I smiled down at Emma and pulled her toward it. "Come on."

We slid inside, not letting any space between us. Emma was smiling from ear to ear. "What?" I asked, smiling back. Her happiness was infectious.

"Nothing," she said, but her smile didn't fade. I squeezed her hand. This was happiness. This was love. She was mine and she was perfect. She was in awe of the surroundings. I couldn't take my eyes off of her. "Have you been here before?" she asked. I swallowed hard and let out a nervous laugh.

"A lot." She smiled again and sunk her body back against mine. I wrapped my arm around her. I didn't want this moment to end. I had too many skeletons, too many secrets. One day she will run from me. Not today, though. Today, she was mine.

We turned off the main road, and I knew we were only seconds from reaching my parents' home. I couldn't help the nervousness I felt, even though I knew they were somewhere on the other side of the world.

The car pulled up to the gate, and the driver punched in the access code.

"Where are we?" Emma asked, craning her neck to see outside. I held her against me. We rounded the fountain in the center of the drive, and the car finally stopped. Our driver came to our door and opened it for us. "Go ahead," I said, her eyes full of excitement. I reluctantly let go of her with a kiss on the forehead, and she slid across the seat and stepped out into the sun. I climbed out behind her and waited for her response.

"This is beautiful." She sighed.

I grabbed her hand. "Come on."

"Our stuff." She motioned to the trunk of the car.

"It will be brought to us," I assured her, pulling her toward the door. She stopped just inside, taking in the surroundings. It was just like I remembered it. The floor was a white marble with a crystal chandelier that hung above. Ahead were two identical spiral staircases. It had ten bedrooms and a bathroom for each. It was completely over the top.

"Overwhelming?" I asked as her eyes scanned the room. She nodded with a giggle. "I figured after the last few weeks we could really use a nice vacation. Come on. I want to show you our room." We made our way up the right staircase to my room at the top. I opened the door and let her pass me. She ran her hand over the post of my bed, and I felt my pants tighten in response. The room was sparse with only the dresser on the far side of the bed. There were no pictures, no momentos. This wasn't my parents' doing. I didn't care enough about anything to keep a reminder of it.

"So beautiful." I wrapped my arms around her waist from behind.

"You are the most beautiful thing in this house." I kissed her cheek lightly. I needed this. I needed every moment with her to be perfect before it all came crashing down around us. I pushed her on the bed playfully and let myself fall on top of her. I traced her jaw with my finger as she smiled back at me. *I will miss this.* I glanced at the wall at the head of the bed.

"What?" she asked, following my eyes to see what I was looking at. I kissed her.

"I was just trying to figure out how to tie you to the posts." Someone cleared their throat behind us.

"Your belongings, sir," our driver announced with irritation in his voice. I nodded at the man. "Are you wanting something for lunch?" he asked. I glanced down at Emma and back to the doorway.

"No, thank you. We will be going out for lunch. Dinner still at eight?" The man nodded and exited the room. Emma cocked her head to the side. I slid off of her reluctantly and held out my hand to her. She took it and I pulled her off the bed. "Hungry?" I asked, wrapping my arms around her back. *Mine.*

"Very," she said, grabbing her stomach. We made our way to the garage where my Mercedes-Benz E-Class convertible still sat. Thank God my mother wouldn't let my father get rid of any of my things.

"You like?" I asked as she beamed from ear to ear. I hit the alarm, and she nodded and slipped into her seat.

We drove across town with the top down, soaking up the evening sun. I took her to one of my favorite secluded restaurants, La Bella. We chose a table by the front window, enjoying the freedom of being able to just be us in front of everyone.

"I could get used to this," she said, and I pulled my eyebrows together wondering what I had done to deserve her. Wondering if money would change her the way it had Abby. She studied my expression and quickly began to explain herself. "I meant being able to be out in public with you. It's nice." She reached for my hand. I tried to look more relaxed, but I couldn't stop thinking about what I would do when the other shoe drops. "What is it?" she asked.

"I know all of this is…fun, but it can really destroy someone's life if you let it." The truth was, money or not, I had already put several nails in our coffin.

"William, look at me. I didn't even know this part of your life existed. I don't care about any of this. I love you." She was trying to comfort me. Money was one thing. What about the club, the deaths, the drugs? I swallowed hard and turned my attention to my food. "Do you trust me?" she asked, her eyes full of worry.

"Of course I do," I reassured her, but I knew she would have no choice to leave me eventually.

"I'm not her," she said quietly. I pulled my hand back from hers and ran it through my hair.

"Let's get out of here. I want to show you something." I didn't want to talk about Abby. I wanted this time to be about us. She smiled and tossed her napkin on her plate.

"Where are we going?" she asked. I stood and took her hand, grabbing some money from my pocket and tossing it on the table.

"It's a surprise."

Chapter Thirty

We drove out of the busy city onto a hilly, wooded road. The top was down, and Emma's hair swirled in her face as the radio blared.

"Almost there," I yelled. She shot me a grin and squeezed my hand. I loved opening up to her like this, letting her in. I wish I could tell her everything. We pulled off the main road onto a dirt drive. After a few minutes of trees, we came to a clearing. I parked the car. "Come on," I said, hopping out and making my way to her. I took her hand and pulled her to my side. We stood on the edge of a massive hill, overlooking the city below.

"This is beautiful!" she said. I wrapped my arms around her from behind and held her.

"This is where I go to be alone. I've never brought anyone up here before." I relaxed against her, committing this moment to memory. Soon it would be all I had.

"It's amazing. Thank you for bringing me here."

I turned her around so I could look into her eyes.

"I know I have some serious trust issues, but I am trying hard to work past them. I hope you can see that."

Her arms snaked around my neck. "I love you, William. I'm not going anywhere. No amount of money in the world could compare to this moment right here."

What about lies? What if the hands I touch you with have also taken the lives of others? I pulled her against me and kissed her head. If I didn't do everything in my power to stop it, she was going to leave me. She just didn't know it yet. The one thing I hadn't counted on was her aunt. There was no avoiding the train wreck that was going to come. I needed a plan. She pressed her lips to my neck, ceasing all of my thoughts. I pushed back against her with my hips. Her lips trailed up to my ear sending a shiver down my body.

"If you don't stop that now, I'm going to have to fuck you right here," I said, but I already knew it was going to happen. She bit down playfully on my earlobe. I gripped her hips tightly and spun her around, placing her facedown on the hood of my car. I needed to remind her again who was in control. Her hands spread out helplessly against the hot metal as I undid my belt. She lay perfectly still, waiting for me. I pushed her skirt up her back and slipped her panties to the side. She was already wet for me. I didn't take time to get her ready for me. I pushed inside of her as she cried out. I fucked her hard and without mercy. She was mine to do with what I wanted, when I wanted. She fucking loved it.

We made our way back to my parents' house much more relaxed. The sun was setting, and it would soon be time for dinner. My phone rang and I contemplated ignoring it until I looked at the caller ID. It was my mother. I swallowed hard and answered the call.

"Yeah?" I glanced over at Emma, who was staring at the scenery.

"William, why didn't you tell us you were coming to town?" my mother asked. She knew why. If I had known they would be there, I wouldn't have shown up at all.

"I thought you were on location."

"Your father wrapped up filming early. He is very excited to see you." *Bullshit.* My father and I never got along. He always treated me like a burden, and my mother never said a word.

"I have to go," I said and ended the call. Emma didn't say a word the rest of the drive. I was glad. I just wanted to get our things and get the fuck out of town as soon as possible.

I pulled up to the house and punched the security code into the keypad. My father's butler was waiting by the door when we arrived. I tossed him the keys to my car and pulled Emma inside behind me. We made our way up the steps, and I closed the bedroom door behind us.

"What's wrong?" she asked, placing her hands on my chest. I glanced down at them and back at her, but she didn't move them. I clenched my jaw but had too many other things on my mind.

"I didn't know they were coming. We can leave right now if you want, get a hotel room?" I ran my hands through my hair.

"Who?" she asked, sounding afraid.

"My parents." I stared at her, hoping she understood.

"Oh," she mumbled, and her hands fell from my chest. "Just take me home." She turned away.

"Hey." I grabbed her arm and forced her to look at me. "I didn't mean to upset you," I said, not bothering to change my tone. She pulled out of my grip, seething with anger.

"If you didn't want anyone to know about me, why did you bring me to your home?"

"I didn't know they would come. My father is supposed to be in Ireland on set for the next few weeks." *Why was she so upset?*

She crossed her arms over her chest.

"It's not that I'm trying to hide you, Emma. I just didn't want to subject you to my father. He's not a good man." She looked me up and down, and I realized how stupid that sounded coming from someone like me.

"William?" my father called from downstairs. I stiffened.

"I love you, Emma. I'm not ashamed of you." I grabbed her arm and pulled her out of the room to the landing.

"There you are." My father called out. He laughed but it was hollow and empty, much like his heart.

"Dad," I said, flinching at the word as it left my mouth.

"Who is your friend?" He grinned at her like a wild animal. I realized I was digging my fingers into Emma's hips. There would probably be bruises later.

"This is Emma, my girlfriend. Emma, this is my father, Gerald Honor." She looked at him for a moment before she realized who he was. Everyone knew my father. He was a very successful director.

"Pleasure to meet you." Emma smiled.

"I'm sure it is," he replied arrogantly.

"Well, come on down and greet your mother. She will be happy to see you." Just then my mother stepped into view.

"William!" she yelled and held out her arms for me. We made our way down the giant staircase, and I gave her a long hug.

"Who is this, dear?"

"Mom, this is my girlfriend, Emma. Emma, this is my mother, Martha," I explained.

Emma smiled and held out her hand.

"Pleasure to meet you, Emma." My mom smiled at her and took her hand.

"Enough of this. Let's go eat dinner," my father said, walking away from us. I gave Emma an apologetic look, and she smiled sweetly back at me.

We sat down at the dining room table and waited to be served. Several servers brought in our plates of food. No one spoke.

"This looks amazing." Emma smiled up at the woman who had placed a plate in front of her. The woman smiled back, but it soon faded as she caught my father's eye. None of the servants looked familiar. It was hard to keep any help around the house with my father's domineering attitude. He treated everyone like they were beneath him, especially women.

"That will be all," he said coldly to her, and she looked to the ground as she quickly made her way back into the kitchen. He shot Emma a glare, and her gaze dropped to her plate. I wanted to leap across the table and strangle him. *Mine.*

"So, how did you two meet?" my mother asked, as she took a sip of wine from her glass. I slipped my hand under the table and rubbed Emma's knee. If she hadn't figured it out yet, my father and mother had a similar relationship to ours.

"At Kippling," I answered, my eyes locking onto my fathers. He held his glass midair for a moment before taking a quick sip and setting it down hard.

"Well, I think that is nice. Don't you, Gerald?" My mother was silently pleading with him to be kind. His eyes danced back and forth between us. His jaw clenched tightly.

"I guess I should get the checkbook," he said coldly and began to cut his steak.

I held Emma's knee tightly, trying to keep her calm. She began tapping it rapidly, and I knew she was biting her tongue. She slipped her hand under the table and placed it on top of mine, rubbing it gently.

"That won't be necessary, Mr. Honor. I, unlike some, don't put money over love." Emma smiled at me devilishly, and I smiled back. She didn't bow to anyone but me.

"Playing hard ball, are we? What will it take, two…three million?" He smiled sadistically.

Emma pushed back, dropping her napkin on her plate. "I apologize, but I need to excuse myself, Mrs. Honor." She nodded understandingly to my mother, who looked like she was ready to cry at the harsh exchange.

"She is not your fucking wife, and you will *never* talk to her like that again." I looked at my mother who sunk down in her chair. Nothing had changed since I had last seen my parents. My mother lived in my father's shadow, under his control. I left the table and rushed to Emma's side. She was already in the bedroom.

"Emma." She was shoving her things in her bag and on the verge of losing it.

"Get me out of here." Her tears began to fall. I wrapped my arms around her and pulled her into my chest.

"I'm so sorry." I rocked her, trying to calm her down. A light knock came at the door.

"Please don't leave like this, William. We haven't seen you in years." My mother looked defeated.

"She's not Abby." I squeezed Emma in my arms.

"I know." My mother smiled, but her eyes were full of sadness. She turned her attention to Emma. "My William is a special boy. Please take good care of him." She turned to leave, pulling the door shut behind her. I ran my thumbs over her cheeks to wipe the tears away.

"Let's get out of here." I kissed her on the forehead.

We rode across town in silence. Emma was still upset, but she was looking less and less angry as we put distance between ourselves and my parents. I hated my father, but it felt good to stand up to him. I wasn't a young naive kid. I was my father's son. Flaws and all. I just hoped Emma never looked at me the way my mother looked at my father.

When we made it to our room, Emma curled up in a ball on the bed. Today had been emotionally exhausting. I slid behind her and kissed her on her shoulder.

"Are you all right?" I asked when she didn't say anything. She nodded. I turned her over to face me, searching her eyes. "What's wrong?"

"My stomach." She sighed and rubbed her hand over her belly. I looked at her for a moment.

"I'll run to the store and get you something for it." I kissed her quickly and left. When I got into the hall, I leaned against the wall trying to calm my racing thoughts. *Could she be pregnant?* My mind raced as I thought of all of the times we had been together. We hadn't used condoms every time. I cursed myself. This was not something I had to worry about with any of the others. I always made sure they were on birth control. I struggled to keep my composure as I went to the gas station down the road to get a pregnancy test.

By the time I made it back to our room, Emma was fast asleep.

"Emma," I whispered, waking her from her sleep.

"What?" She rolled over and rubbed her eyes.

"Get up."

"I'm not in the mood." She waved her hand at me and buried her face in the blanket. *What the fuck?*

"Get up now." I was nearly growling. I pulled her into the bathroom and turned on the light. She recoiled from the sudden brightness. I slapped the test down on the bathroom counter.

"What is it?" she asked, her voice sounding scared. I didn't care. I ran my hands through my hair and struggled to keep my composure.

"It's a pregnancy test."

"But I'm not…I mean…I can't be." She was stuttering and on the verge of tears. I was sick with guilt. It was only a matter of time before Emma found out the kind of person I really was. Bringing a baby into that situation was fucked up, even for me.

"Now!" I yelled. She jumped and grabbed the test. She did as she was told. After she returned the test to the counter, she pushed past me. A few seconds later, I heard the door to the room open and slam shut. She was gone. I didn't chase after her, just stared into space and waited for the five minutes to pass so I could read the results.

Time practically stood still. I went into the main part of the room and began emptying the minibar of all of its contents. I had lost count of how many drinks I had as I stumbled back into the bathroom. It was hard to decipher if there was one line or two with the double vision I was seeing. I closed my eyes and steadied myself. When I reopened them, it was finally clear.

One line.

She wasn't pregnant.

Relief swept over me but was quickly replaced with guilt. I had pushed her away. I was so worried about everyone else that I ended up being the one to destroy everything. I sunk down on the floor and wallowed in my self-pity until I passed out.

I awoke stiff and heartbroken. I jumped to my feet and checked the time. Only a few hours had passed. I logged onto my phone and did a search for Emma. Her GPS placed her at the airport. My stomach twisted in knots. I called to book a flight, but they didn't have anything else available, so I made plans to use my father's private jet. I called my mother and made sure it was all right.

"Fix things with her, William," my mother encouraged me.

"If she will have me. Thanks, Mom," I said and hung up. I hurried to make it to the airport.

I didn't try to call Emma. I needed to see her face-to-face. I needed to see her, even if it was for the last time.

Chapter Thirty-One

I would make it into town a few hours after Emma. I checked my watch constantly, trying to keep myself from calling her. The flight seemed to last forever.

When we finally arrived at the airport, I checked Emma's location. It put her at a location I didn't recognize. I drove as fast as I could across town.

When I was only a few minutes away, I tried calling her.

"She doesn't want to talk to you. You missed your chance," a man's voice said. The line went dead.

I felt like someone had just stabbed me in the heart. She was with another man. I called back, trying to think of anything but my Emma in someone else's arms. There was no answer. I was dying. I hit redial. It rang twice before she answered.

"What?" she slurred angrily.

"What's wrong with you?" I growled. I couldn't think straight.

"What is wrong with me?"

"Are you drunk?"

"Hey, if you need a shirt or something, I can grab you one of mine," a male voice called in the background.

"Who the fuck was that?" I yelled, demanding an answer.

"My friend," she spat back.

"I'm five minutes away. Come outside *now!*"

"How did you…" Her voice trailed off.

"Here," the male voice said, very close to the phone. Very close to my Emma.

"Thank you," she replied to him.

"I think you should lie down." His voice was so crisp and clear, I knew he was practically on top of her.

"I'm fine." She sounded panicked. "I said I'm fine! Get off of me!" she screamed.

I threw the car in park and opened the door to the building she was in. It banged loudly against the wall. I could hear her screaming from behind the door to apartment A. I shoved the door in and ran down the hallway.

I grabbed the man who was laying on Emma and slammed him against the wall. His head snapped back and cracked against it.

"Mr. Honor?" Jeff slurred, confused. I drew back and punched him as hard as I could. Blood sprayed from his nose. I grabbed his shirt and pulled his face close to mine.

"If you *ever* hurt her again, I will kill you." I stared him in the eye to make sure he knew I meant it. I would have killed him right there if it wasn't for Emma. I turned and held out my hand to Emma. She slipped her fingers in mine. I grabbed her things and pulled her out to the street. As soon as we reached the sidewalk, she lurched forward, vomiting all over the ground.

"Well, I guess you know that you're not pregnant," I said quietly. She looked at me for a long minute.

"I knew all along," she replied angrily. I opened the car door. "Let's go."

She slid in and waited for me to join her.

"Just take me to my car." I looked over at her, but she stared out of the window. I stepped on the gas and headed across town. I wasn't going to let her leave without having a chance to explain myself.

Chapter Thirty-Two

took her to my place. She was angry, but I needed to take care of her. I got her a towel and set the water so she could take a nice warm shower. As she cleaned herself up, I made her a sandwich to help soak up the alcohol.

She ate quietly, barely even glancing my way. When she was finished, I took her plate into the kitchen. She sat on the couch with her knees drawn to her chest. I took a seat next to her.

"I want to go home."

"Give me a chance to explain." I said, trying to hide my panic. She glared at me. I swallowed hard, trying hard not to show her how pissed off that made me.

"What is there to say?"

"I know you deserve better than me." I looked at her and waited for a response. She didn't say anything. "Can I hold you?" I asked, desperate to feel her against me.

She didn't move.

I slid closer, wrapping my arms around her. I know she wasn't happy with me, but she didn't pull away. I laid her back and sighed, trying to find the right words. I pushed back the hair from her face.

"Abby was pregnant."

Her body stiffened against me.

"What?" She twisted toward me but didn't pull away.

"We had just found out." I smirked inwardly at how odd it made me feel.

"You have a..."

I shook my head no before she could finish her thought.

"She took the money, remember? She didn't have room in her life for me and our..." My voice trailed off. Drugs and money were the downfall of my world. "I'm sorry I didn't tell you. I just...couldn't." A lone tear escaped my eye.

She took her thumb and wiped it away. The thought of how my life could have been was something I rarely let myself dwell on. It was too painful.

"I'm so sorry," she said quietly.

I ran my hands through my hair. I couldn't lose Emma too.

"*You're* sorry? Emma, I damn near ruined your life in the short time that I've known you."

"William, everyone has a past. Mine isn't that great, either. Yours made you who you are today. The man I love." Her hand slid across my chest to my heart.

"You still love me?" I couldn't see how it was possible.

"More than anything." She smiled as her eyes drifted to her hand on my chest. "I belong to you," she said quietly. I grabbed her hand and held it tightly against me.

"I love you more than anything, Emma. I don't want to ever feel the way I did when I thought I had lost you forever."

She smiled and leaned in to kiss me. I pressed my lips hard against hers.

Mine.

"Marry me."

~The End~

About the Author

I was a Russian spy at the ripe age of thirteen, given my uncanny ability to tell if someone was lying (I also read fortunes on the weekends). By sixteen I had become too much of a handful for the Lethal Intelligence Ensemble (L.I.E.). I was quickly exiled to the south of France, where I worked with wayward elephants in the Circus of Roaming Animals and People (C.R.A.P.). I was able to make ends meet by selling my organs on the black market for pocket change and beer money. At the age of twenty-three, I decided to expand my horizons and become a blackjack dealer in Ireland. I loved the family atmosphere at Barney's Underground Liquor Lounge (B.U.L.L.). People couldn't resist the allure of liquor up front and poker in the rear. Eventually I became tired of the rear and headed off to the United States to try my hand at tall tales. That is what brings us here today. If you have a moment, I'd like to tell you a story.

(This bio is not to be taken seriously under any circumstance.)

Teresa Mummert is an army wife and mother whose passion in life is writing. Born in Pennsylvania, she lived a small-town life before following her husband's military career to Louisiana and Georgia. She has published the Undying Love Vampire Series, Honor Series, and *Breaking Sin*. She also contributes to SocialSex.org. Check out her website for samples and updates!

http://www.teresamummert.com

Please read on for an excerpt of *Honor and Obey,* next in the Honor Series.

Honor and Obey Excerpt

by
Teresa Mummert
Chapter One

*M*y thoughts were spinning out of control, and I gripped William's hands tightly in mine until the skin of my knuckles turned white.

"Marry me," William repeated, his eyes burning into mine.

My words caught in my throat, and I suddenly had the urge to flee.

"What if…what if someone found out? What if you lose your job?" My voice was panicked, and I was practically yelling.

He placed his hand on my cheek and stroked it soothingly. I closed my eyes, trying to calm myself down.

"I don't care about any of that anymore. When I almost lost you, I realized what was important to me. I don't ever want you to leave my side again." He pressed his lips against mine, begging me to say yes. I got lost in his touch for a moment but quickly regained composure.

"I can't ask you to do that," I said, placing my hand on his chest.

His heart was beating wildly. His muscles flexed under his jaw. "You didn't ask," he replied, his words sharp, and I could tell he was on the verge of losing his patience.

"I'm not saying no." My voice was barely a whisper. I wanted so badly to jump in his arms and scream yes from the top of my lungs, but I couldn't be the reason he lost everything in his life. He would eventually regret it, and, in turn, he would regret me. His body pulled back from mine. I put my hands on either side of his face and stared him directly in the eye. "I want to marry you. I just need some time. Take things slow," I said, forcing a small smile.

William's hands met mine, and he squeezed them gently. "That's all I want," he said, wrapping his arms around me and spinning me around.

I couldn't help but let myself get lost in his happiness. I squeezed his neck tightly and buried my face in his chest, breathing in his musky scent. When I thought about all we had been through—the ex-wife, the jealous girlfriend, the even more jealous husband of said girlfriend, and the horrible way William's father had treated us—I couldn't even begin to imagine how others would take the news of us being married.

I wanted to run away with him. I wanted to forget about Florida and all of the trouble that had come along so far and just get lost with him. But, I knew that was impossible. Even with all of the money in the world, and William did possess quite a bit, we could never hide from everyone forever.

William kissed me softly, lingering just above my mouth, leaving me craving more. The mood around us shifted from panic and excitement to pure lust. I slipped my fingers up his neck into his hair. His hand twisted into a knot in my hair, tugging gently.

"Never leave me, Emma," he whispered.

"Never," I replied. His mouth found mine, hard. His tongue pushed gently against my lips, and I let them fall open for him. His other hand slid down my spine and over my bottom, squeezing gently. I let out a quiet moan into his mouth. His hand moved further down my thigh and rested below my knee. He pulled my leg up to his side as his breathing became heavier. I wanted more than anything to feel his flesh against mine, to rid my thoughts of all that we had endured. I tugged feverishly at his belt as my body ached for him. I cried out as he pushed the length of himself into my thigh.

"I want you," I breathed heavily as dampness pooled between my legs. He shoved me back onto the couch and quickly undid his shirt. I was completely caught up in the moment, sliding my hand down my thigh toward my most sensitive areas.

His eyes burned with need as he threw his shirt to the ground and quickly undid his belt and slipped his jeans down his legs.

"Take your clothes off." His voice was low, and his eyes traveled down my body as he spoke. I bit my lip and slipped my T-shirt over my head, revealing my bare swollen breasts. His jaw clenched and I continued, pulling off my shorts and panties as I lay back on the couch. I rested my hand just below my belly, running my fingertips over my skin.

"Show me how badly you want me." His words sent a shiver down my spine, and my fingers automatically responded to the seductive sound of his voice. I slipped my hand lower, my fingers gliding effortlessly across my wetness. I let out a breath as I felt my insides tighten. William's hand mirrored mine as he slowly stroked himself. "You are so beautiful." With his words, I became bolder, dipping a finger inside myself, my back arching in response.

"Oh, God," I panted as he lowered himself onto the couch.

"Don't stop," he instructed as he traced the entrance of me with his hardness. I began to rub harder as he slipped the tip of himself inside, causing all of my muscles to tighten in response. I wanted him inside of me, deep inside of me, and I was willing to do anything he asked.

His fingers found mine, and he slowed my movements, making my hand move in smaller, more deliberate circles. He rocked his hips slightly, just enough to tease my body. I let my free hand slide over my breast, my nipple hardening under my fingers the way he had made it do before. I pinched it gently as his eyes wandered over my body. My hips rocked against my hand, and I was struggling to control my breathing. "Does that feel good?" he asked, and I could barely find my voice to answer.

I nodded, my lips parted.

He slipped himself in a little further, and my body reacted, grabbing him and trying desperately to pull him deeper inside of me. I raised my hips, silently begging him to slide in deeper, but he held firm. "That is enough of that."

He grabbed my wrists and pushed them over my head. I lifted my hips again, desperate to find my release. He responded by pulling out of me completely. He repositioned himself so that he held both of my hands in one of his and slipped the other down between my legs. He slowly dragged the tip of his finger up and down, barely touching my skin.

"William, please." I cried out, tugging against his hand. He dipped a finger inside of me suddenly, nearly sending me over the edge, his mouth just inches from mine as I panted.

"Please," I moaned, and he slipped a second finger inside, angling just right to touch places inside of me that I didn't even know existed. I rocked against his hand unable to stop myself. I widened my legs, making sure he could have a clear view of what he was missing. He took his thumb and slowly circled over my most sweet spot as his fingers continued to slide in and out of me. "Oh, God." I turned my head, pressing it against the cushion.

"Look at me." His breath tickled my ear. I turned to look him in the eye, breathing in his sweet, minty breath. "You wanted to take things slow."

Look for *Honor and Obey*, available on Amazon and Barnes & Noble!